12 TA
MANHOOD

A FATHER & SON TREK

JACK A TAYLOR

Book and Cover design by Blake Arensen, Old Africa
Cover Photo by David Peters, Unsplash

ISBN: 979-8488-0348-7-7

Dedicated to past and future
12 Taskers committed to transformation

CHAPTER ONE

The late spring sun glistened off the North Shore mountains and streamed across the harbour onto sea planes, cruise ships, passenger ferries and freighters as it lit up the sky-scraper jungle that formed Vancouver's downtown. The thirty-second level of a prominent bank building with floor to ceiling windows unveiled the wonder of Stanley Park, the Lion's Gate Bridge and the glory of creation all around.

A lone figure knuckled his chin and turned from the view. "Deal!" he said. Vincent Lau reached across his desk and vigorously shook the hand of another happy customer. Overseas money was pouring into the city and he was making himself a key funnel for it into the real-estate market.

As he escorted the new owner into the waiting arms of an associate, who would handle the paper work, his smartphone was already ringing. Fifteen minutes later he pocketed the device and looked out at the skyline. "That should move me back into number one," he announced to no one in particular.

A knock on the door interrupted his reverie. Jessica, his personal assistant, bounced in. The Brittany Spears look-alike, a recent grad with a passionate commitment to cycling and pickle-ball, had been his first hire. "Tim Wong is waiting for your late lunch," she said. "Stratford deal. I've got the folder here."

Vincent looked at his driftwood wall clock and calculated his travel time. "Tell him I'll be seven minutes late. Order lunch, drinks, whatever it takes. I've got the tab." He adjusted the framed pictures of his wife and son and lined up his pen straighter on his jotter.

"I'll text you the afternoon schedule," Jessica said as she exited.

The successful real-estate executive grabbed the folder and headed to the elevator for a trip down into the private parking garage. The elevator seemed to stop at half the floors with everyone vacating for lunch. Of all things, in this imitation sardine can, a woman with heavy perfume stood right in front of him. His nostrils closed down in protest. Even his eyes watered and a slight throb began to put a vice-grip on his temples. Where was a Covid mask when you needed one? It didn't pay to have asthma.

For seventeen floors he endured before she finally vacated. By the time he reached his BMW, his shoulders were knotted and his neck was guitar string tight. He inhaled deeply at the oasis of comfort which now surrounded him. The smell of leather was a balm to his airways.

The powerful engine purred to life and Vincent eased it into drive. He spoke the name of the restaurant and watched the map display light up the screen on his dash. He'd miscalculated what ten minutes late could mean for traffic jams on these streets at lunch.

His transfer to this metropolis had come after years of proving himself in the suburbs for his father's firm and he'd moved here deliberately on the west side among the office towers paying tribute to the dreams of numerous global architects. The estranged relationship with his dad was not something he wanted to focus on when everything else was turning around for him.

The mortgage on his west-end home would probably kill him if his work schedule didn't first. Or, if his marriage lasted through the tension of a new neighbourhood. The traffic inched forward then came to a halt. Three car lengths from the street he needed there were bodies filling the roadway. He opened his door and stood to view the hold-up. Some insane protest group had launched away from the Court House steps to snarl up the traffic and make their point known. A tumble of dark cloud slid overhead to block the sun.

He stood at the side of his car and used his smartphone to contact his lunch appointment. "Tim, yes. Vincent here," he said. "I'm stuck in a protest rally by the courthouse. Any chance of delaying this a few minutes? They shouldn't be long."

Just then, the driver of a black SUV behind him blasted his horn and made an attempted U-turn. The right bumper of the vehicle crushed the tail light of his BMW on its way around. Vincent felt a twinge in his back as the door he was leaning on lurched away from him. He regained his balance, dropped his phone onto the driver's seat and yelled at the escaping vehicle which kept right on going. Two other vehicles quickly followed suit in doing U-turns and racing away.

Other drivers, caught around Vincent, vacated their cars to sympathize and express their own outrage. A few police officers arrived and prevented other cars from turning around. One of the officers looked at the damage on the BMW and called a tow truck. Vincent insisted he had to go, but all he got was a shoulder shrug.

The tow truck still hadn't found him by the time the protestors were cleared away twenty minutes later so he decided to sort things out himself. He knew a mechanic from church who had his own shop. He could probably get a deal there.

He called Tim Wong back again. "Tim, Vincent here." He tried to sound cheerful. "I'm finally free. Hope you haven't eaten everything yet."

His face and voice betrayed the feedback he was getting. "Tim, can we reschedule?... If he's got to get to the airport right now, I can meet him there. ...." He slammed his hand on the roof of his car. "No, Tim, Rick isn't the man for this deal. ... C'mon, it was just a few minutes...." He combed fingers through his close-cropped hair. "Yeah, I know. Cut throat. Fine. I'll be there for you next time."

The frustrated real estate agent scrolled to his calendar for what was coming next. He had two hours. Just enough time to zip over to the shop and get the light repaired. A drop of rain splattered on his windshield.

Traffic was decent, now that he was away from the downtown core, and now that the lunchtime crowd was dispersing back into the underground parking garages. He noticed that he even reached 20 on his speedometer on one stretch before he hit another red light.

It was 1:27 when he pulled into his destination. Maxwell's was all the painted sign at the entrance said. It wasn't much to look at as a building. Two slide-up doors with open grease pits. Only one old Honda up on the hoist. He celebrated his good timing with a double honk to alert the owner.

The two had met at a church men's breakfast the first week Vincent had moved into town. The ambitious real estate baron wanted to get into a good worship center and build

4

his contact list. Jettisoning from his father's firm, after being overlooked in promotions, he needed to show the old bull that he could make it on his own in the most challenging market around.

The mechanic he sought had been the first to greet him at the door of the church and to introduce him around. Everyone just called him 'Njoroge'. The man had a solid grip and a contagious smile. He'd been in Canada six years already. The fact that the two of them had sons the same age helped with the bonding.

Vincent was standing behind his BMW, examining the shattered light, when the establishment owner ambled out and chuckled.

"Jambo, Bwana. Goo'day Comrad. Hello, Mr. Real Estate," he trumpeted. "Looks like we're going to need something more than duck tape to deal with this one."

Vincent straightened up and was greeted by the wide toothed smile of Maxwell Njoroge. The mechanic had the build of a rugby prop with a cauliflower ear to prove it. "I can't believe I lived in Langley for five years and didn't have a scratch," he said. "This is the third time I've been dinged in my first six months here."

Maxwell was quick with his reply. "If I'd only had three dings in Nairobi in six months I'd be celebrating. It was like a demolition derby over there."

Vincent put out his hand and endured the vigorous hand pumps. "I need it done in an hour. I've got a really important appointment at three."

Maxwell chuckled again. "Important appointment. I had one of those once. I think it was my wedding day."

Vincent smiled. "Okay. So maybe this isn't the biggest day of my life, but I still need the car done in an hour."

Maxwell pulled out a small notebook and jotted something indecipherable to Vincent's watching eye. "I'll see what we have in stock." He held out his hand as more rain drops fell. "Why don't you take a look at the magazines? I think I've got a few that I saved from the trash a few years ago. The headlines will still sound like it happened yesterday."

Vincent took the time to review some of his upcoming client appointments and then scanned the room for the coffee machine. He was looking for a cup when Maxwell ambled in. "Looking for Coffee? – fresh, last Friday! – sorry, ran out of paper cups and customers keep forgetting to bring their own. Anyway, we're out of stock."

Vincent stood still under the onslaught of words and tried to absorb the implications. "What am I supposed to do?"

"Depends what you'd like to do," Njoroge said. He pointed at a map of his homeland on the wall. "Safaris are good this time of year in Kenya."

"How long will it take you to get the part?" Vincent insisted.

Maxwell scratched his head above his right ear. "Special part? BMW. I know the dealer." He picked up a dog-eared parts catalogue. "Tomorrow for sure. Let me check the computer to see what's available."

As Maxwell pecked away at the ancient computer keyboard, Vincent's phone vibrated in his pocket. He looked at the call display. His wife! He answered. "Yes."

Her Scottish lilt floated across the airwaves and he held the phone slightly away from his ear. His face squinted as she

6

continued on and on. His only comments made it clear that things weren't going well on the other end. "Yes... today?... now?... not again!... why can't you do this? ... what's wrong with that kid?... okay... okay... we need to talk about this... okay... bye."

Maxwell stepped away from the computer. "Trouble?"

Vincent eyed the mechanic. "My son is in the vice-principal's office again," he admitted. "I don't know what has gotten into that boy. My wife is out in Abbotsford shopping with her friends. She wants me to get to the school. I don't understand women." He spread his hands out, palms up. "We move to the city with all this shopping and she has to travel an hour to go to the stores she used to go to."

The shop owner tapped his key board a few more times. "I can't help your marriage or your fathering right now, but I can tell you we'll have the part by noon tomorrow."

Vincent paced across the office. "I don't want the rain getting into that break and I don't want to duck tape it up and make it look like some cheap auction special."

Maxwell tossed him a set of keys. "Take mine." It's a Honda and I have an extra set of those. They'll copy anything at the mall." He backed away. "Bit old, but it runs and gets you where you want to go." He chuckled. "No GPS. Nothing automatic. But the tail lights aren't broken. Just bring it back when you can."

Vincent hesitated as he looked around the lot. "Thanks, is it close?"

Maxwell laughed again. "It's on the hoist. Gotta make sure there's room in the parking lot for customers." He headed for the bay. "I'll get it down. And don't worry about me. I can take the bus from here."

Vincent stepped outside and waited for the car to be lowered.

Maxwell backed the old Honda out of the bay and stopped it near Vincent. "All yours! The wipers mostly work but you need a key to get in. Sorry, no fob." He hesitated on his way. "God's best with your boy. I'll be praying."

"Thanks," Vincent said as he opened the Honda door. "I just wish I knew how to help that boy. This is just such a hard place to help kids grow up."

As Maxwell reached for the door to shut it Vincent heard his reply. "I know what you mean."

CHAPTER TWO

Vincent beat out a tune on the steering wheel at a Tim Horton's drive through until his phone rang. It was his personal assistant with a call being transferred from his son's school. He was past the stage of superstition in life, apart from his sports teams, but he knew instinctively that trouble came in threes.

He numbly allowed the transfer call to happen and greeted the vice-principal.

"Good afternoon, Mrs. Tsang. I don't suppose you're looking for a good deal on a home? It seems like we've talked a lot lately."

He listened for a minute and then played his part in the conversation. "Yes.... I understand.... No.... His mother isn't available today...." He turned down the radio. "Yes.... Are you sure it's him again? Stephen's always been a good kid. Straight A's. No trouble." He nudged forward to place his order. "Do you think he's being bullied? It can be scary for a new kid starting middle school." He listened but covered the phone to place his order.

Three minutes later, Vincent sipped his Ice Cap and glanced at his appointments. Two showings in the later afternoon. One this evening. If he had to give up another of these to his competition, he'd be slipping even further in the company ratings. Maybe he could do this quickly. "I'll be there in twenty minutes," he told the vice-principal. "I'm under a lot of time pressure so please keep it short."

One glance out the window at the storm clouds assured him that the rain would only increase. 'Go figure!' The weather outside was a perfect reflection of the weather inside.

He abandoned the Honda in a handicapped space in the school parking lot and Vincent rushed through the gaggle of students ogling their cell phones on the stairs of the school. 'Kids don't even talk to each other in person anymore,' he muttered. 'How's a new kid supposed to make friends?'

His neck and tight shoulders threatened to make him scream when he finally reached the main reception desk. The secretary saw him coming and motioned him through Mrs. Tsang's door. Stephen was seated in a corner with his head down.

A flashback of himself in a moment of shame hit him with the force of a bull. He sank into the waiting chair and turned away from his son toward the administrator.

"You know this needs to be quick."

Mrs. Tsang opened up a file and read. She finally looked up. "We're talking about Stephen, your son, Mr. Lau."

The shame ran deep, but Vincent refused to look away from her stare. The administrator finally backed off and explained the reality of the situation. "Stephen hasn't turned in any assignments for three weeks now," she began. "He is dozing off in class and he is refusing to participate in group discussions. The staff haven't seen him making any friends and they wonder how things are going at home."

Vincent turned in his chair and stared at his son for the first time since entering. "Is this true?" he asked. "Are you staying up at nights and playing those video games and not doing your assignments? Don't you care about your reputation? What are people going to think of you?"

Stephen cowered in his chair and Vincent felt a mixture of revulsion and compassion at the sight. 'What was a father supposed to do to help his son in a situation like this?' There were too many regrets from his own relationship with his father that he didn't want repeated. 'But what chance was there of that?'

Mrs. Tsang stood up behind her desk and drew his attention back to her. "I would like to speak to you alone for a minute, if I may. I think Stephen can wait out in the main office until we're through."

Vincent did not appreciate being humiliated in front of his son and he stood when his son did. "I think I'll just go with him and take him home."

The administrator raised her hand in a 'stop' motion. "If we don't settle this today, then I think Stephen will need to take a few days at home to think about what he really wants at school."

Vincent used every personal skill he could embrace at that moment to keep his anger under wraps. He ushered Stephen into the office and then returned back for a half hour of intense conversation with the administrator who seemed to be holding his son hostage.

As he rose to leave the office his phone vibrated. It was his secretary, Jessica reminding him that he was ten minutes late for his appointment. "Give them some paperwork to fill out," Vincent said. "I'm just wrapping up with my son. I'm 30 minutes away. Stall.... Yes, I know that the developer will be there by then.... Jessica, what am I paying you for?.... No, do not let Rick handle them.... Well, tell him to go talk to his own clients.... Yes. I'm on my way."

When Vincent pocketed his phone, he looked up to realize that everyone in the office had frozen in place as they watched him in action. His son, Stephen, was once again cringing in the corner.

Mrs. Tsang stepped up to his side. "Are you always this intense?"

Vincent looked around again at each person who was staring at him. He nodded politely, as he knew he should, then moved to sit down beside Stephen. "I'm sorry, Stephen," he whispered. "Please forgive me. It's been a tough couple of days and I just need some time to figure things out. Are you okay to go home now?"

Stephen sloughed off of his chair without a word, grabbed a green back pack which Vincent assumed was his, and marched out the exit without a backward glance.

Vincent caught up with his son at the outside doorway and held the door with the heel of his hand for a few young girls who were still texting their way out.

When they reached the parking lot Vincent saw Stephen hesitate. He realized that his son didn't see the BMW and didn't know what to do. "I had an accident," Vincent said. "The car's in the shop. Toby's dad lent me his car until tomorrow. It's that blue Honda over there."

As the two of them made their way across the parking lot a young Latino boy jogged up and fell into step with Stephen. "Hey, big man," he said. "Masters of the Universe. Level 10. Kiss the world good-bye."

Vincent watched his son brighten for the first time in weeks and the two boys exchanged a fist bump and shoulder punch.

"Who's your friend?" he asked his son.

"Alejandro."

"Where do you live?" Vincent asked. "Do you need a ride?"

The boy looked up as if seeing Vincent for the first time. "I use the skateboard express," he said. "Thirty minutes of air-cooled luxury."

Vincent looked at Stephen. "It's raining. We'll get you home dry."

Stephen actually looked up at his dad and smiled. "Really? I thought you had appointments."

"Thanks for reminding me," Vincent said as he stopped and pulled out his smartphone. "Jessica, cancel my appointments, I'm not going to make it. Maybe Rick can take care of them just for today."

CHAPTER THREE

Stephen seemed to lose his voice and enthusiasm for life the moment Alejandro slammed the door of the Honda and stepped off onto his skateboard. The two boys had erupted during the short ride like verbal volcanoes without once paying him notice. The only thing they could talk about was their video game successes. "What? Am I the invisible man?" he joked from his driver's seat, but even this didn't get a response.

As he pulled into his driveway, the real estate agent noticed his wife Margaret standing by her Mini Cooper in the drizzle talking on her cell phone. The passenger door was still open and the bounty of purchases was obvious. He wondered why she didn't just shut the door instead of trying to cover everything with the blue and white golf umbrella she was trying to control in the stiff breeze. She was laughing with whoever was on the line, but he knew that this wasn't really an indication of what was going on in her world.

Vincent cringed as the Honda door slammed before he had even turned off the engine. Stephen gave a weak wave to his mom and sauntered through the open garage and into the kitchen entrance. He knew the puzzled expression on Margaret's face meant that he would need to have a good story about the car. For the moment, he knew that her finger pointing at the passenger door meant that his current purpose in life was to haul in the latest supplies.

The realtor was proud that he managed to wrestle everything into the kitchen in only three trips. He couldn't fathom why this weekly phenomenon didn't rate him a significant number of brownie points but he was happy for the peace it kept.

During his trips to the car, he caught on that Margaret was discussing school issues with someone. This certainty kept him from dragging Stephen back out to help with the task of bringing things in. Who could understand a son who never seemed to have time to assist with things around the house? What was happening with this generation?

He was in his den checking emails when Margaret strolled in and gave him a peck on the cheek. He accepted her cheerful "thanks" and reached back blindly to grab her hand. All he felt was the swish of her skirt as she twirled on out.

"Who was on the phone?" he called.

"You'll have to come in here if you want to talk," she said. "I'm putting away the groceries."

The surge of negative energy in his chest added to his sense of righteous indignation. 'Why did his wife always have to have her way? Didn't she realize how much pressure he was under to raise the income to finance her little shopping extravaganzas? And why wasn't she focusing on Stephen more?'

He quickly sent off replies to two urgent emails and then grudgingly heaved himself out of his office chair. Margaret was crouched down, busy emptying bags into the vegetable drawers in the fridge.

Vincent took a deep breath, consciously counted to three and tried to calmly engage. "I said, who was on the phone?"

Margaret didn't even look up as she continued her work. "Oh, that was Navid Samadi. He's the staff rep from Stephen's school who works with me on the PTA. Poor guy! He's having such a hard time with his son, Darius." She handed him an empty bag and continued her task. "His wife died of cancer two years ago and he's teaching at the school to try and provide for his three kids. His oldest son is so angry that he's become a bully and always seems to be in trouble. They used to go to church, but things have gotten so complicated they're kind of on their own." She handed over another bag. "His parents are still in Iran and his mom has been so sick lately. I've been trying to encourage him not to give up. He's such a good teacher." She straightened, shut the fridge, and leaned against the kitchen island. "He's even offered to come here and tutor Stephen in his Math. I wish you could motivate Stephen to take him up on that."

"I'm not sure Stephen is too keen about anything but video games right now," Vincent said in defense of himself.

"Where's the car?" Margaret asked.

"Don't you even want to know what happened with Stephen and Mrs. Tsang?" Vincent said.

"Of course," Margaret said. "But why are you changing the subject?"

"Someone smashed my tail light and I had to take it in to Maxwell's to get repaired. Njoroge let me have his Honda while he's waiting for the part."

"Isn't that sweet of him," she said, opening a cupboard. "How's Toby doing these days?"

Vincent stepped toward his office. "How am I supposed to know?"

She closed the cupboard and moved toward him. "You were talking to Njoroge weren't you?"

"Of course!" He stepped back toward her.

"Then how could you not know anything?" She adjusted the hand towel on the stove handle. "What do you men talk about?"

"I went to get my car fixed," he said. "That's what we talked about."

Margaret pivoted on her toes and then stood up in Vincent's face. "No wonder you are all having trouble with your sons," she said. "You could help each other if you just got together. What's more important? Your cars or your sons?" She reached for the coffee pot. "Maybe you should all go talk to Pastor Harris about how he managed to raise his son so well. It seems to me that boys need their dads. Life is complicated."

"Since when is this parenting our son all about me?" Vincent asked.

"It just seems to me that boys nowadays are missing out on something. There's no consistent markers anymore to tell them how to be men or what it even means to be a man." She sipped her coffee. "I've seen guys in their thirties who seem to still be stuck in their boyhood. If anyone knows how to tell a boy how to be a man it should be his father."

"Times have changed," Vincent said. "I don't think my dad understood me anymore than I understand Stephen. It's just the way it is. Stephen just wants to play video games with Alejandro. How am I supposed to help him with that?"

She set down her mug. "I just think fathers should find some way to get to know their sons."

"Look at the mess King David had with his own sons," he argued. "Even Adam had one of his sons kill the other. How's a father supposed to change human nature? It's always been this way."

"Don't you think that someone should try and change the trend?" She opened the dishwasher, withdrew the plates and set them on a counter. "If your dad couldn't help you and you can't help Stephen then what are our grandsons going to end up like?"

"Every generation has a different way to tell how a man is a man," he insisted. "Some people have bar mitzvahs, some have circumcision ceremonies, some have special ordeals. We have things like driver's licenses and graduation."

Margaret fidgeted with a cloth bag and emptied a dozen jars of spices on the counter. As she looked at the labels and sorted them, she added her response. "It seems to me that being a man is about more than just what is happening to you or around you. When I think of a man, I think about who he is. His character, his personality, his ability." She folded the bag and set it in a drawer. "Surely a father can impact some of these things before his son is unleashed on the world to drive a car and find a job. By the time those things happen it seems to me that it might be just too late."

Vincent set his hip against the kitchen island. "You'd think that the schools would figure all that stuff out. That's where boys spend most of their life."

"I'm sure all kinds of places and people can make an impression on our son," Margaret said. "You can leave it up to a coach, or a teacher, or a pastor, or a neighbour, or someone on television. Somehow, it seems to me that who a boy's father is, and how a boy's father is, makes the biggest impression."

18

He crossed his arms on his chest. "What's that supposed to mean?"

Margaret picked up a broom and swept the floor. "Just what kind of an impression did your dad make on you and how is that still affecting you? And what kind of an impression are you making on Stephen and how is that going to impact him for the rest of his life?"

Vincent turned to leave. "I don't have time for this?"

"I think you've hit the nail on the head," Margaret said. "Your son needs you and you're too busy to even notice."

CHAPTER FOUR

The call came a week to the day after Vincent had turned away from his wife's rebuke and gone for a one hour walk around the sea wall at Stanley Park. The realtor was in his home office, busy surfing his MLS listings so he let the answering machine handle the message. Margaret was away at a women's Bible study group and Stephen wasn't back yet from his afternoon with Alejandro.

Vincent was so focused on his task that he didn't realize who the caller was until the phone had switched to voice mail. He recognized his uncle's voice speaking in Cantonese. There was a sense of urgency and sorrow in the vague phrases he tried to interpret.

He reached the phone just as the message finished and by the time he picked up the mobile unit his uncle had gone. He waited for the blinking light to start and pressed the message button. He let his mind do the work as his heart constricted in pain.

"So sorry to inform you about your father," his uncle said. "We will make arrangements until you come. This was all too sudden. We will wait for your call. You can see our number."

The meaning of the message was all too clear but the realtor played it over again twice more to confirm his interpretation. He sat and stared at the phone, unable to command his hand to do the task that had to be done.

Vincent was still sitting in the same place when Stephen walked in and sat in front of the computer. He was still perched there when Margaret walked in and called out her cheery greeting. His throat seemed to choke off any words he wanted to say.

Finally, Margaret walked into the den. "It's nice to see you two in the same space. What's going on?"

Stephen gave his typical response as he continued his video game. "Nothing."

Margaret was about to turn when she noticed that something more than nothing might be going on with Vincent. "Honey! What's wrong?"

Vincent could only point at the answering machine and Margaret pushed the button. She could hear the tone of the message but she didn't understand Chinese so she asked her husband to explain.

"Dad is dead. I have to go to Hong Kong."

"When?" Stephen asked.

"Tonight!" Vincent said. "I have to go tonight."

"I'll help you pack," Margaret said.

"I'll book your flight," Stephen said. "Do you have your credit card?"

Half an hour later Vincent slouched in the passenger seat of his wife's car with a boarding pass neatly pressed inside the pages of his passport. Just two years before, his mom had passed away. Now his dad was gone too. It seemed harder to breathe.

His father had been vigorous, stubborn and aloof as ever for the first month after his mom's funeral service, but after that he resigned from his business and moved without warning back to Hong Kong. The company had been handed over to another realtor without even a discussion with Vincent. Very few words had been spoken in the time since and now the chance for words was gone.

The phone call with his uncle Hang had been brief, confirming his fears. His dad's heart had given out not too long after he had given up on living alone. His dad had forbidden any phone calls during his two-week hospital stay. As the oldest son, Vincent had to come immediately to do his duty.

The long flight gave Vincent time to reflect on his family heritage. His grandfather had been one of the Chinese survivors during the Japanese occupation of Hong Kong in the Second World War. Margaret's great-grandfather before that had been one of the British administrators in Hong Kong after establishing himself as a tea merchant in the developing city. It was this common thread in ancestry that had helped bridge their differences as they began a relationship through their years of study at the University of British Columbia.

Vincent knew his dad had sold his Vancouver house and bought a small apartment for the same price in Aberdeen, Hong Kong. The flight was 14 hours and he was exhausted by the time he arrived. An airport taxi took the realtor on a one-hour journey along Sky Plaza Road, onto routes 8, 3, 4, 1 and finally onto Yue Shi Cheung Road. Uncle Hang was waiting for him.

For ten days life was a blur. In that blur there was only numbness. Faces, places, papers, signing, traditions. On his last day he revisited several of the parks and harbours where he and Margaret had traipsed during their honeymoon fifteen years previously. He tried to take pictures so his wife could see the changes.

And then it was done and he was back on the 14-hour flight back to Vancouver.

Margaret and Stephen were both at the airport. On the way home Stephen spoke up from the back seat. "Dad, what was grandfather like?"

Vincent was surprised by the question. "What do you mean?" he asked his son. "You know your grandfather."

Stephen was persistent. "I know he sold a lot of houses and he hardly smiled at you. He gave me lots of gifts."

Vincent looked sideways at Margaret for help but she deliberately looked out the passenger window. His tongue felt swollen and difficult to manage. "Your grandfather was a good man," he finally said.

"I'm not asking what kind of man he was," Stephen responded. "I want to know what kind of a dad he was."

Vincent tried to find words that would honour his dad yet speak truth. "Your grandfather worked hard to provide for his family," he started. "When we came to this country, he had to work even harder to deal with a whole new way of running a business. We always had what we needed."

"But did he love you?" Stephen asked.

The question was like a harpoon to his heart. "Different fathers show love in different ways," he answered. "My dad showed love by making sure we had what we needed."

"Did you feel like he loved you?"

"I really don't know how to answer that question," Vincent admitted. "He was my dad. How am I supposed to feel?"

Stephen kept up the conversation. "While you were gone, mom showed me the family photo album of what it was like for you growing up," he said. "I saw a lot of pictures of you and grandmom but not a lot of grandfather. The only time you and he were in the same picture was when he was showing you a little telescope and a compass."

"I'll admit, I had a hard time with my dad," Vincent said with intensity. "That telescope was his attempt to teach me astronomy. Every night he was home he would make me memorize the star charts and take that telescope outside to see the stars." He weaved around a slowing bus and accelerated past a taxi. "We lived in the city. You can't see stars in the city." He floored it through a yellow traffic signal. "He also tried to teach me about Chinese herbal medicine. We have doctors for things like that. I feel like he stuffed my head full of useless information. Even when he taught me about real estate – it was all useless information."

Margaret interrupted him. "Vincent! You've just come from burying your dad. Stephen needs to honor your dad's memory. He doesn't need to hear any more about why you didn't get along with your dad."

Stephen spoke up as if there had been no interruption. "Did grandfather believe in God?"

"Faith was important to your grandfather," Vincent answered. "He was just very private about the way he showed it."

"What did you say about your dad at the service in Hong Kong?" Stephen continued. "I kind of wished I could have been there. I don't feel I had the chance to say good-bye."

"I've got a copy of what I said in my suitcase. You can read it when we get home," Vincent said. "I don't really feel I had the chance to say good-bye to him either."

CHAPTER FIVE

The six-a.m. call caught Vincent off guard and he bolted up in bed as he reached for the phone. It was Njoroge from Maxwell's. "Cock-a-doodle-doo Mr. Real Estate Man. The flock is out here working for chicken scratch and the day's a wasting," chortled the melodious African voice. "Just reminding you that your tune-up and brake service is scheduled for eight-thirty. Are you operating on west coast time yet or is your body still over in Hong Kong?"

"I'll be there if you promise to keep the grease outside the car this time," Vincent teased. "Did you get a chance to drive the Beamer last time I left it with you?"

"Nothing like a Beamer to impress my lady," Njoroge responded. "And the kids. For one day people looked at me like I was somebody. I was going to let Toby take it for a spin but I figure twelve is still a little young to be getting into demolition derbies. I promise you this time I'll take my coveralls off before taking it to the drag strip."

"I'll see you in a couple of hours," Vincent said. "Is that your rooster I hear crowing in the background?"

"I was just about to wring his neck for breakfast," Njoroge answered. "If you get here in time, I can spare some of the innards for you."

Two hours later, Vincent was surprised to see several other cars already positioned for service. He had never seen Maxwell's this busy before. He recognized the Blue Audi as belonging to Navid and sure enough the math teacher was seated in the waiting room as he entered. An old blue 64 Corvette was on the hoist and a white pickup nestled up against the fence.

Vincent was greeting Navid when Njoroge walked out of his office with Pastor Peter Harris. The pastor immediately took the initiative greeting Navid and then turned to Vincent. "My condolences on the loss of your father," he began. "You've reminded us again about how important those relationships are between father and son."

"Morning, pastor," Vincent said. "Sounds like Njoroge's been talking again too much."

"Not at all," pastor Harris replied. "Some of the younger fathers at church were lamenting how hard it is to help their sons become men. Njoroge just let me know that you and he had been talking about something similar. We've been talking about getting together to brainstorm on what could be done for any of the fathers and sons who might be interested."

"Njoroge is one of your best salesmen," Vincent said.

"I'll grant you that," Peter Harris agreed. "And talking about salesmen, I was just remembering that it was your father who sold my brother his home in the valley. Jim said that your dad was one of the most thoroughly prepared salesmen he had ever met. Knew every house he showed inside out."

"That would be my dad," Vincent acknowledged.

Njoroge broke into the conversation. "I was telling the pastor that back in my day we had initiation ceremonies where the older men brought together the older boys for a month of special teaching and events and when we were done we knew we were all age mates that didn't have to face life alone anymore."

Vincent smiled. "Yeah, I read about that kind of stuff in National Geographic. I think there are a few boys who would not be wanting to participate in what you went through. I like the idea of initiations though. I've heard of some people who tried to teach their sons about passages of life like the old knights used to go through."

"You might be interested in something I took my sons through," pastor Harris said. "We called it our 12 Tasks of Manhood. We found it was good for both our family and our community. In fact, my son Michael is preparing to set something up for his son Matthew in the next few months. We could all get together and see what you think about it."

"Don't kids get their family and community on the internet these days?" Vincent asked. "It seems all I see these days are kids texting or chatting with their friends on computers. No one talks face to face anymore."

Njoroge jumped back into the conversation. "Look at us. Doing something new. Talking face to face. Man to man." He grasped Vincent's shoulder and smiled. "If these kids don't get into relationships with anyone more mature than they are how are they going to grow up? These internet communities aren't real and they won't last. Those machines are sucking the real life and character out of our kids. They're missing out on our values and beliefs and the things that make us belong to each other. If there's one thing I miss in this country it's this sense of community and belonging. I don't want my son to grow up feeling even worse."

Navid stood to his feet and approached the trio of men standing by the counter. "I couldn't help overhearing your conversation about initiating sons," he said. "My son is also 12, like yours. I'm having a terrible time trying to figure out how to help him become a man. Is this group exclusive or can someone like me join you?"

Njoroge was the first to embrace Navid in a bear hug. Navid stiffened, so Njoroge stepped away and gave him a few back slaps. "Man hug," he said. "Gotta practice that one on your boy."

"Anyone's welcome," pastor Harris said. "Let me have your card. I'll figure out a time with the others and let you know what's happening."

Njoroge stepped into the middle of the group. "I've got work to do if you are ever going to get your cars back," he said. "Pastor, Vincent's office is on the way for you if you could take my courtesy vehicle and drop him off. Navid, you'll be done in 30 minutes if you can wait. All those students need their teacher looking good today."

On the way to work Vincent asked the pastor to explain the 12 Tasks a little more. Pastor Harris responded. "I think I'll get Michael to give you his side of things when we all get together. We actually got the idea from another missionary who was doing it with his sons. We just modified it for our kids."

"Can you tell me anything about it?" Vincent asked.

"Well," the pastor said, "the main purpose of the 12 Tasks is to help your son discover some of his key strengths, key growth areas, and key life skills so that he gains a sense of confidence in who he is and who God has designed him to be. It's also a great bonding time for fathers and sons as they work through the 12 Tasks together during the year."

"What was it like for you as a father with your son?" Vincent probed. "How did you convince your son that doing these things would help him become a better man?"

"It's hard to remember back that far as to what I exactly said," pastor Harris replied. "I'm sure it has a lot to do with the way you present the whole thing. You have to know your boy enough to have done the work so that he can see you want the best for him. He also has to see that you're going to be in this with him and that it'll be as good for you as it will be for him."

"Sounds like a challenge," Vincent said. "Let me know when you're meeting. I've got a lot of work to catch up on since I've been away. I'll try to be there if I can."

The rest of the day at the office for Vincent was an overwhelming foray into piles of manila folders which his secretary, Jessica, had managed to collect and protect while he was gone. "I'm afraid Rick picked up a lot of the clients that were up for grabs," she told him. "You're now running about eighth in sales. I've scheduled both of us for overtime meetings the next two weeks to try and catch up a little."

Vincent expressed his appreciation and felt the adrenaline surge through his body. He'd been so weary with all the focus on Stephen's struggles and on his dad's death. These few files meant that there were people waiting on him to do what he did best. To find those sweet deals and special homes for overseas customers which would boost his own commissions and keep the peace at home. This was going to be a long day.

The next four days meant leaving his office after mid-night and even on Saturday he was into work before seven in the morning. Two of the nights found him pacing in the kitchen talking animatedly into his cell phone at 3 am in order to add that personal touch with a prospective buyer in another time zone in China.

The first time Vincent saw Stephen that week was at nine on Sunday morning when he tried to encourage his son to get up for church. He had debated long and hard about whether he could afford the time off but a few tense conversations with Margaret on Saturday convinced him he needed to focus at least a few minutes on something apart from work.

Maxwell Njoroge was the first one to meet Vincent in the foyer at the church. "Jambo, Bwana, Mr. Realtor, Beamer Buddy, we missed you and your son yesterday. I thank God you are still alive. Oh, by the way. Welcome to The Door. When you're open, we're open."

Vincent wasn't sure what meeting he had missed and his face betrayed his confusion. Maxwell picked up on that. "The father-son thing with pastor Harris," he said. "I left you messages at your house. Don't tell me you didn't get home this week."

"I've actually been working late and early every day," Vincent said. "Trying to catch up. I'm afraid I didn't even listen to any messages at home."

"Hakuna Matata, no problem, house-man," Maxwell chirped. "If you get really good at this house selling thing, my auntie has about eleven mud and dung houses in Kenya that could use a buyer. They're fixer uppers but the view is great and the climate is warm."

"I'll take a pass on that," Vincent said. "What did you guys talk about yesterday?"

"It was just me and the pastor and Michael so we didn't do a whole lot," Njoroge said. "We were hoping for a few more dads to get some momentum. Michael was just talking about what he was doing for his son Matthew. I'm kind of psyched. I was telling my son Toby what I went through to become a man in Kenya and he wasn't quite into it so I think this could be a good option for here."

The two men separated to join their families for the service and didn't see each other afterward. Instead, it was Michael Harris who caught Vincent at his car in the parking lot. "Vincent, I hear you're interested in being a part of our father-son 12 Tasks," Michael said. "We'll be meeting again next Saturday if you want to join us. My dad and I are just going to explain how we did it and how we're setting it up for Matthew."

Vincent shook the extended hand and worked hard for the right words. "It sounds interesting, Michael," he said. "I need to talk it over a bit more with Stephen to see how it works for him and I need to check on work. As you know, I had to take quite a bit of time off to deal with my dad's death in Hong Kong and I'm behind and working hard to catch up. If I can't make it this week I hope we'll be able to connect real soon. That 12 Tasks sounds like a great idea."

He had hardly closed the car door when Stephen spoke up from the back seat. "What are you trying to get me into now?" he asked. "You may think 12 Tasks sounds like a great idea but you haven't talked to me about anything in the past week. I think we both know what's important around here."

CHAPTER SIX

It was Thursday evening before Vincent finally felt he was getting his head above water. That, and the guilt of abandoning his family, gave him the courage to leave the last twelve files on his desk and send Jessica home at seven.

When he got home, he found Navid seated at the dining room table with Stephen working through some Math problems. He waved his greeting and went straight to the den where Margaret was sitting at her laptop answering emails.

"Since when did we invite someone else to tutor Stephen?" Vincent asked.

"Good to see you too, honey," Margaret said. "I talked with you about this before you left for Hong Kong. Stephen is desperate for help. Navid was willing so I asked him. Someone had to be there for our son."

Vincent felt the familiar surge of anger rising up from within but pressed his lips together and determined not to say anything to make matters worse. He'd left work deliberately to be with his family and now all that he was getting was more guilt. He flipped on the computer and buried himself in his work.

Navid stopped by an hour later to bid his farewell and Vincent got up to walk him out the door. "Thanks for what you're doing for Stephen," he said as humbly as he could.

"I just wish I could do the same for my son, Darius," said Navid. "Sometimes it seems easier to help boys who aren't your own."

"Doesn't seem right, does it?" Vincent stated. "Are you still interested in that father-son group with pastor Harris? They're meeting this Saturday."

"Just tell me the time," Navid said. "I've got a few things to do around the yard and I'll need someone to watch the kids if I go."

Vincent felt a little more connected to Navid after their farewells and began to look forward to the upcoming get together.

An email the next day let him know the event would be at Michael Harris's home at two in the afternoon. He noticed that the message was also sent to Navid, Njoroge, and three other fathers who had boys just shy of thirteen years old.

The Saturday event arrived fast. The first twenty minutes were spent with introductions. In addition to Michael, pastor Harris, Navid, Vincent and Njoroge there were Samuel Ortiz, Jesse Browning, and Hanny Prakash. "The all-nations team," Michael pronounced.

Pastor Harris led the meeting with a question. "When you think of your boys becoming men what characteristics do you want others to see in them?" He handed out blank sheets of paper. "Why don't we write these down and learn from each other."

"Honesty and a commitment to truth," Njoroge said, accepting the paper and searching for a pen. Michael handed out pens around the circle.

Jesse lifted his hand. "A sense of duty and respect." The men wrote that down.

"Confidence, peace with who they are, hope for the future," Hanny added.

"A purpose for their life, no regrets," Vincent said.

"Anything else?" pastor Harris asked. "We're getting quite the list."

"I want him to feel like he belongs somewhere," Navid said. "I want him to be settled and loved."

"And how in our society will boys become this way?" pastor Harris asked.

Michael spoke up. "As a dad I have to tell you I'm wondering that myself," he said. "I see that every message Matthew hears is telling him that he has a right to do whatever he wants, to take whatever he pleases, to choose whatever he feels like regardless of how it impacts others. I can't see how he'll ever get past thinking about himself if someone doesn't give him a reason to think differently."

Samuel added his thoughts. "I've seen that our boys seem to be struggling not only in school but in the community," he said. "It seems that boys need someone older to come alongside them and encourage them to explore their world and to use their strengths in a responsible way for the good of the community. They need some kind of direction to help them understand where their sense of expertise might be. They need someone to believe in them, to have faith in them, to stand with them through the challenges they'll face."

"So, you think that fathers are supposed to do all that?" Navid asked.

"Not alone," Michael responded. "In community – with others like us. But yes, we should be the first one in line helping our boy become a man." He taped his list on the wall.

"Sounds like we're setting up some kind of tribe or ancient

fraternity," Jesse said. "I'm not into anything freaky and I don't want my boy getting overloaded with everyone setting up things he can't hope to do."

"That's the beauty of the 12 Tasks," Michael said. "When my dad set this up for me, we sat down together and came up with four tasks that focused on strengths that he saw in me. We set up four tasks that focused on helping me grow in areas that weren't so strong in me. And we set up four tasks that we could do together to improve our skills and relationship. The other men were the encouragers and sometimes the mentors but dad was always the first one in line to see me through."

Pastor Harris spoke up. "Within each of us, God has designed a strength, a power, that will find a channel for release. This release will define who we are and what our place in this world will be. If that power or strength doesn't get channeled it can easily end up in abuse or it could be lost all together. This power can influence others for good or bad. It can perform positive things or negative things. Boys are looking for meaning and value and purpose and they'll move toward anyone who is giving it to them."

"That's a scary thought," Jesse said. "That's why gangs are so effective in recruiting our boys."

"Don't you think sports teams or groups like scouts can pick up some of the slack for our boys?" Hanny asked.

"Not all boys are athletic," Vincent said. "A boy can get lost in a group where everyone is forced into a common mold. I agree that this individual mentoring and attention is essential to helping a boy transition successfully to manhood. I think that's what I missed out with my dad. I can see that he was trying to do something. I just didn't know what. I think whatever we do has to be clearly understood by the father and the son."

"Again, that's the beauty of the 12 Tasks," Michael said. "Both the father and the son work out the tasks in a way so that they understand the purpose and the expectations of what will be done during the year. There's a timeframe and a plan. There's support and encouragement and then celebration at the end. And if the boy knows he's not the only one doing this - that there are other boys in his community striving for their own manhood - then he knows he's not alone."

"He also knows that his father isn't weirder than every other father he knows," Njoroge added.

"Sometimes I think the reason why boys love their video games so much is that it gives them a sense of power and choice and accomplishment which they don't get in the real world," Michael said.

"I feel sometimes that our boys think that we don't value them and that they have to prove their value somehow," Samuel said. "I think that's why they get into trouble with girls or drugs or gangs. They have to prove themselves to someone."

"What are they trying to prove?" Jesse asked.

"That they're someone worth noticing," Hanny replied. "That they've got what it takes to earn the respect of whoever will notice. That they've got power and they're using it."

"I think our boys really need to know that we are noticing them and that we want to help them become men worthy of respect in our community," Michael said.

Navid cleared his throat and waited until everyone looked in his direction. "I've read a lot of anthropology and there are a lot of groups that do this kind of stuff intentionally. They all seem to have some kind of disengagement period where the boys ready to become men are identified and set apart some way. Then there is some kind of deliberate challenge that works as a transition step. There is a lot of learning that happens at this phase. When the boys successfully conquer the challenge then they're relabeled or given some new responsibilities or privilege or recognition."

"That's what I'm talking about," Michael said.

"Let's bring the boys in next week and see what they think," pastor Harris said.

CHAPTER SEVEN

Vincent went into work a little later on Monday. He wanted to make sure he said good-bye to Stephen in the morning before school. If he was going to convince his son to come on Saturday, he would first have to gain some ground in connecting and communicating.

He still had his coat half way off when his boss, Shepherd walked in through his door. "Vince, sit!" he barked. "We need to talk."

Vince finished taking off his coat and slumped into his office chair. Shepherd towered over him. "I know you tried hard after Hong Kong to get back on top of things," he said. "But you're down to sixth in sales and you're starting to hurt us."

"I was first for three months in a row," Vincent said defensively.

"And that's where I expect you to stay," Shepherd said. "Rick is making you look like a rookie. It's your commission but it's ours too. I need you to head to Tokyo this weekend and get some traction for our group. The following weekend I need you in Singapore. This business is about networking and I need my top guys where the action is."

"I was making some plans with my son for this weekend," Vincent said.

"It's your neck, Vince," Shepherd warned. "I only have so much office space here. If you want it, I need you to earn it."

"How about Hong Kong or Beijing again?" Vince asked.

"You can stop by there on your way through if you have

active contacts," Shepherd said. "I just need to see those files piling up."

Margaret didn't take the news of his trips very well. Vincent left an email for the men in the group a few hours before heading to the airport. Stephen was away at Alejandro's so he still hadn't talked to his son about the 12 Tasks before leaving.

The trip was a whirlwind of handshakes and sales pitches and lunches. Once he got into the groove Vincent knew he hadn't lost his touch. The results were encouraging and he was satisfied by the time he touched down in Vancouver ten days after leaving. He hadn't even reached home before Shepherd was on the line asking him how he'd done. The pressure was intense and he could feel it in his neck and shoulders.

The tension increased when he walked into the house and set down two of the latest video games next to Stephen at the computer. He had picked them up specially in Hong Kong. Stephen looked at the covers and non-chalantly tossed them onto a pile of others he had collected.

"I thought you'd like those," Vincent said. "They're new out in Hong Kong. They're not even here yet."

Stephen put his head into his hands. "When were you planning on telling me about these 12 Tasks?" he asked. "Somehow Darius and Toby and Alejandro and Matthew and Jimmy and other guys all had talks with their dads. They even had a meeting and talked about us. How do you think I feel when I have no clue what's going on? What kind of a dad are you anyway? Trying to buy me off with video games."

"I've got a job, son," Vincent said. "I had to go."

"You've got a family, dad," Stephen responded. "Maybe you need to get a different job."

Vincent was still sitting at his computer long after Stephen had walked out of the house. Margaret eventually arrived home and welcomed him without much enthusiasm. He could feel the pressure cooker inside about to blow and he took time for his own walk to cool down.

Two days later Vincent arrived home to find Stephen intently working on Math problems with Navid. He almost turned to walk out of the house but Navid stood up and came to him.

"Vincent, your son is showing amazing improvement," Navid said. "We have to talk about the 12 Tasks. The group met again this past Saturday and we all agree that you and Stephen should join us."

"It's probably too late," Vincent said. "I've missed three meetings and I haven't even had the chance to talk with Stephen about the group."

"The other boys have been talking with Stephen," Navid said. "Even Darius is willing to be part of this. We've all started drafting our first four tasks focusing on the strengths of our sons. You can still do this. I brought you a copy of something I got from pastor Harris at the group. I think it's worth thinking about. It helped me buy into what they're doing."

Vincent accepted the double-sided sheet of paper and looked past Navid at his son who was watching. "I'll read it," he said. "You better finish what you're doing with my son."

In the den, Vincent laid out the sheet and began to read.

TRANSITIONING

Changing from boyhood to manhood is a larger transition than some of us anticipate.

Whenever change happens it inevitably leads to chaos in some form. Before transition happens, life seems predictable and comfortable – at least familiar. You know where you belong, what your role is, how you're known and accepted, and you know how life works – at least you think you do.

Fathers have usually figured out something of what fathers are supposed to do and sons have usually figured out something of what sons are supposed to do.

Enter adolescence and change.

Once you step out onto the bridge of transition you may find it feels more like a poorly secured suspension bridge than a solid footbridge. The rushing rapids of change may be swirling below and create a sense of anxiousness and fear for those unfamiliar with the terrain.

Both fathers and sons may feel a sense of uncertainty as life adjusts from total dependence of the son to a level of independence and then to interdependence. Fathers or sons may be tempted to back away and try to entrench themselves in what they have become familiar with. If either the son or the father is ready and the other is not, resistance may be acted out in a subtle struggle that will not be comfortable for either.

The role of the 12 Tasks is to assist fathers, on the suspension bridge of change, to adjust from their comfortable position of leading in the front, where they alone set the pace and example, to a relationship where they can support their sons with encouragement from close behind. Something big changes when a boy finds himself setting the pace across an unsteady transition.

The 12 Tasks are positioned to come right in the middle of the time of unsettledness. The Tasks help focus the anticipation, anchor the routine of change, provide support during the times of grief, and establish confidence toward what is still ahead.

Pre-adolescence often straddles times of changing schools, friendships, internal emotions and life interests. A sense of internal confusion, instability with unfamiliar desires and urges, fears of the unknown, and an unexplainable urgency for more independence and new opportunities can magnify the impact of stress, problems and uncertain friendships.

The 12 Tasks help build confidence as personal values are solidified, as new roles are embraced or discarded, and as new routines are established and acknowledged by those who are significant to the newly emerging young man.

WHEN EVERYTHING IS CHANGING IT'S GOOD TO HAVE SOMEONE COMMITTED TO BEING WITH YOU.

STICKING POINTS

There are three things a son will need in order to complete his journey through the transition phases. He will need hope for the future, confidence in the present and peace with the past.

Peace with the past. In order to achieve peace with the past a boy needs to know that there is forgiveness for his mistakes and there is healing for his wounds. While the mistakes and wounds may not be significant after 12 years of life, it is crucial that forgiveness and healing are clearly applied to whatever level of experience has occurred. While this peace with the past can be solidified through the 12 Tasks it is important to be aware of this potential sticking point in the preparation phase.

If a son feels anchored to the past then he will exert strong resistance to stepping into such an unstable phase of transition. While forgiveness and healing will be lifelong pursuits, there needs to be a solid taste of these realities during this phase of life.

Confidence in the present. In order to achieve confidence in the present a boy needs to feel like his closest relationships are secure and that his identity is established. A vital part of the 12 Tasks is to assure him of the security of relationship he has with his father and to assist him in the establishment of his identity as a young man.

If a son is overwhelmed by insecure relationships and an uncertain identity he may become emotionally stuck in this phase. Many of the young men growing up in the chaos of dysfunctional homes and unstable parental relationship can be set up to struggle past this stage.

Hope for the future. In order to achieve hope for the future a boy needs to believe that genuine opportunities for success are available to him. He also needs to believe that he is developing the skills needed for what he will be facing in *the years to come. The 12 Tasks are intended to provide this sense of hope.*

If a son cannot believe that the opportunities before him are within his grasp and if he cannot believe that the skills he has been given in life are enough to help him with the challenges ahead, he will wither. In time, he may choose alternate forms of acceptance or belonging in an effort to belatedly prove himself.

Groups and individuals who prey on the vulnerable seem to have an instinct for younger men who are stuck without confidence or hope. The 12 Tasks can be a valuable aid to protecting young men while they are growing through their vulnerabilities.

When both father and son have peace with their past, confidence in their present, and hope for their future, there will be a strong unbreakable bond that will positively impact the relationships and society around them.

Vincent laid down the document on his desk and hung his head. If only his own father could have provided this peace with the past, confidence in the present and hope for the future. How was he supposed to pass on what he had never experienced himself? It would take a miracle of God and some real soul searching and commitment. In the morning he would have to have a long talk with Shepherd.

Settled - You're back on land with stability, peace, contentment and you experience a new "normal" in your daily life, surroundings and culture. You have gained a new self-awareness and enjoy new values and lifestyles, you have an established role and have become rooted with others and you're able to endure the hardships of that country as a fellow pilgrim rather than a stranger.

CHAPTER EIGHT

The weary father got his first break at the office. Jessica informed him that Shepherd and Rick had gone on a joint venture to Mumbai and New Delhi. He had a week to set his own pace and a chance to pick up a few loose clients that the others wouldn't be available for. The phone was already ringing so he picked up his cell, stepped to his office windows, and began to sell the city that lay stretched out all around him.

Saturday seemed to arrive within a few heartbeats. Each morning had left him feeling like a jack-in-the-box springing up to bounce through his agenda. There were so many voices ringing in his ear and so many files being dumped on his desk that the weekend was an oasis to catch his breath.

Stephen was ready by noon so Vincent took him through his favourite fast-food diner and then for a stop at a local park.

Vincent was digging into his bag for fries when Stephen spoke up. "Dad, I don't think I can do this."

The anxious father settled for snatching a couple of the potato fingers and tried to wait without overreacting.

Finally, Stephen continued. "Dad, do you really think I can do these 12 Tasks? Do you think you can do the 12 Tasks?"

Vincent turned toward his son. "Let's take a walk. I think I have a lot more confidence in you than I have in me. I never got to do this with my dad but the more I hear about it from the Harrises the more I wish I had. All I know is that I want you to become the best man you can possibly become."

Stephen walked along in silence for several moments and then stopped to face his dad. "What do we have to do?" he asked.

The father and son talked over Stephen's strengths and came up with a list of 8 possibilities to build a task around. When they reached the Harris home by two o'clock Vincent could see that most of the others had already arrived. Navid and Darius were standing on the porch talking with Michael and Matthew.

Darius leaped down the stairs in three bounds to meet up with Stephen. "Stephen," he called. "Did you hear we're starting up a 12-14 Ultimate league at the church? Matthew's dad is going to coach us. I'm going to be asking my dad to somehow fit this into one of my 12 Tasks. Maybe we can team up on something?"

Vincent was surprised to see Stephen respond so positively to a young man who used to bully him but he was learning that there were a lot of things that could happen when fathers and sons took the time for each other.

Vincent noticed that there were several fathers who were quick to give out hugs and most of the boys had no trouble receiving them. Other fathers gave handshakes or head nods or shoulder punches. The boys adapted. He himself was more of a head nodder.

The meeting finally got started after he had endured hugs from Njoroge, Michael, Sammy and Jesse.

Pastor Harris was facilitating things again. "Last time we said we were going to focus on four areas of strength for your sons. I encouraged you to try and find eight or ten or even more areas of strength and to do it together. Were you all able to do that?"

Amazingly, everyone had completed the task and Vincent was glad that he and Stephen had taken the time at the park with the list. This was Stephen's first chance to meet with the whole group and it would not have been good to leave him humiliated right at the start. He was glad for the other boys who had talked things up with his son.

"Let me review the chart I showed you last week," continued pastor Harris. "Vincent and Stephen, I don't think you saw this. Let me quickly go over it again."

Vincent looked at the simple diagram on the page he was handed.

Encourage Strengths	Build Relationship
1	1
2	2
3	3
4	4
Learn New Things	**Stimulate Growth**
1	1
2	2
3	3
4	4

"This is just a work sheet to get us started," said Peter Harris. "We're focusing on the strengths section today to help us build up tasks. The other three sections we'll handle in the weeks to come. The titles speak for themselves. We'll work on this together. If you've brought your list of strengths for your son then we're ready to move on."

Michael took over the lead. "Now, what we're going to do is to take time in pairs of fathers and sons and see if anyone else who knows you can add to that list of strengths. We'll rotate every five minutes until you've had a chance to sit with everyone. I want the fathers to explain each time why they believe this is a strength of their son."

"What if the son doesn't think it's a strength even after that?" Darius asked.

"If at the end, either father or son does not agree that this is a strength," Michael answered, "then you can cross it off. If you do cross it off however it will immediately be transferred over to the next section which is our growth areas. If something isn't a strength then it's a growth area to be made stronger."

"But that's next week," pastor Harris said.

"When we're done rotating," Michael continued, "we'll break back down into our individual father-son groups and try to think of a significant task that could be done over a one-year period which would really bring out this strength even more. If you're really good you might be able to combine a couple of strengths for each task. You're going to want to end up with four tasks for this area and it might seem to be good to combine as many strengths as possible into each task. If you can focus on four main strengths, however, and keep it with one task for one strength, it will make things easier on both of you."

An hour and a half went by so quick Vincent was amazed when Pastor Harris called for their attention. "Some of you are well on your way and some of you have more discussion and refining to do. Right now, I'd like to share a few readings from my journal during the time I took Michael through his 12 Tasks. I just want you to see that there are some significant personal things that both dads and sons will be facing. Michael will take time next week to share a few of his journal entries. I just want to give you a little model of how you could keep a record of your adventures together. Each of you should have your own journal if possible."

The pastor opened up a faded, dog-eared red notebook to a marked page near the beginning. "Here are two of my entries," he began.

Choice of Tasks: When I first started thinking through the challenge of choosing tasks for Michael to do, I quickly established that part of his character development would already surface if I chose a larger menu of tasks from which he would have to choose. His ownership of the 12 tasks would come in his choice of what he would do.

Now, there were four tasks which I set down as mandatory. They included one from each of the categories which I was presenting. Climbing Mount Kenya focused on a physical challenge. Memorizing the Sermon on the Mount focused on his intellectual ability and touched on a spiritual challenge. Writing a book touched on his literary and creative skills. Building a tree fort focused on his mechanical skills and on his character.

The tasks were designed to focus on perseverance, patience, self-confidence, creativity and ingenuity, communication, interdependence, personal faith, trust, respect, truth, self-control and self-discipline. Some of the tasks exposed natural passions, interests and skills. Some revealed hidden abilities or character traits. The 12 Tasks are part of the journey of self-discovery.

He looked up. "That was the first entry. Now, for the second."

It is my firm belief that God placed us in a world of relationships to help us to grow deeper in our awareness of who we are and what we are called to do here. In a marriage, a man discovers issues of character at a deeper level than he sometimes cares to know. Yet, in a committed and affirming relationship like this, he is free to explore and discover and deal with his flaws and build on his strengths.

When a man has children, the depths of discovery go deeper still. He discovers levels of tenderness and gentleness and frustration and impatience deeper than he can believe. He learns to sacrifice and to make choices which aren't always in his best immediate interests. He gains perspective about a world bigger than himself.

Interacting with a son who is becoming a man can be another step of self-discovery for a father. Michael was as much a 'young bull' as any other blossoming man. The path toward independence involves a natural challenge of the 'old bull'. Affirming the independence without overreacting to the immature attempts at manhood is an important skill for a father in releasing his son to grow up.

Vincent wondered if he could write journal entries anywhere close to this. His old insecurities wrestled inside him. He couldn't wait until next week. He had to ask now.

CHAPTER NINE

"**B**ut what if you set one of these tasks up and it backfires on you?" Vincent asked. "What if we fail as fathers?" Pastor Harris looked up from his notebook and nodded thoughtfully. "You probably will fail somewhere along the way if you make these tasks challenging enough," he said. "Life is a mix of failures and successes. Part of your role is to teach your son how to keep living in the middle of that mix. Let me read you one entry when I failed with Michael."

Facing Failure: One of the most agonizing moments with my son was when I realized that I couldn't do the very thing I had asked him to do. Some tasks are very event specific and time specific. Climbing Mount Kenya was one of those.

On the day we reached Shipton's cabin for the last stop before summiting Mount Kenya I had used up all my physical reserves. We were just 700 metres short of our goal at Point Lenana. A short scramble up the scree before sunrise for a few hours would finish this task, but it might as well have been a million marathons for me on this day.

Too many people die on this trail so we had taken the night to acclimatize. We had successfully made it up through stunning U-shaped glacial valleys. We had gone through dense bamboo forests with signs of elephant, through the rich montana forest and heathland and then past the strange looking Giant Lobelias and Senecios plants. The peaks of Batian, Nelion and Lenana provided breathtaking images once we broke through cloud cover. Our guides had urged us forward with their steady chant of "take another step, it's just there."

Foundering Reputation: Climbing a mountain when you've had the flu may not be the wisest choice, but this day had been set, the money had been paid, and I wanted to give it my best shot. I felt like my fatherhood was on the line. Other fathers before me had done this and other fathers on this trip were ready to go.

The night's rest didn't settle my heaving stomach. Not having been able to take in any nourishment for the first two days didn't help either. When the call came to summit, early in the morning, I couldn't even lift my head off of the pillow. Sometimes, will power can only take you so far. The group delayed as long as they could, but I was going nowhere.

Depending on others: The other men assured me they could take care of my son. Brian, Mark and Matt were all trustworthy friends. And yet, this is the vulnerability of manhood. Admitting that sometimes others can take your son to places you aren't able to go yourself.

And they did. They piled extra blankets on me and forged out into the darkness.

There is an agonizing sense of failure that can wash over you despite how many good reasons you may have for falling short of the dreams you had. All I was left with were dry heaves and a body frozen to the core. Although I would summit on another trip at another time to prove I could, to summit with my son was all I wished for on that dark morning.

Lost memories: Part of doing these tasks was for the purpose of creating bonding and memories of things shared together. With my failure to emerge for that final climb, we would forever have a gap in our shared experiences and memories. At least that's the way I felt when I wasn't heaving.

My son went up in the darkness as a boy and came down in the light as a man. This volcanic giant, which geologists believe had once been the highest ice capped peak in Africa, had been conquered.

When the victorious men and their charges returned sometime later in the morning the next test arose. The entire mountain had to be descended that very day and there was no way I was doing it on a stretcher. I gained strength from my son's accomplishment and we made the downward trek together. Sometimes the one who you had hoped to provide strength for becomes the strength that you yourself need.

Once again the rock hyrax scrambled for cover as we stumbled past. The cape buffalo watched defiantly on the lower slopes. The Kikuyu and Embu porters delivered us safely to our lodging. While I was awarded a certificate with the rest, I knew that the missing last 700 metres to the summit with my son was significant in my heart.

One of the beauties of the tasks is that whether there is success or failure on the father's part, there will be bonding and memories which neither son nor father could anticipate. When I see the picture of my son raising his arms in celebration, and believing that he finished the task for the both of us, it still brings tears to my eyes.

*My wife claims I looked like death warmed over when I
stumbled in, but my son was triumphant. While the picture
of his victory would often leave a pit in my stomach at my
own failure to escort him all the way, it somehow makes his
completed task more special. He did it without me then, just
like he will have to do many more things without me in the
future. And while he did it without me, he didn't do it alone.
Somehow, I know, this makes a difference.*

"I don't think I could ever write a journal like that," Vincent
said.

"That's what video cameras are for my friend," Njoroge said.
"A picture is worth a thousand words and a moving picture is
worth a million."

"Next week I want you to polish up your four tasks for
strengths and come up with a list of growth areas we can work
on," pastor Harris said. "If you need help, call Michael or
anyone else in the group. We're in this together."

Vincent stayed behind as others began to leave. Stephen was
off talking to Matthew and Toby. "I think my big fear is that
these tasks are going to undermine my son's confidence in who
I am as a man," Vincent said. "I'm not sure I'm really going to
be doing him any favours by trying to get him to do things I
can't even do. Do you have any journal entries about stuff you
weren't good at?"

Pastor Harris smiled. "I'll read something and let you
decide." He shuffled through the old red notebook, found his
place and began to read again.

"Tree Fort: For some of you, a hammer and saw are a comfortable part of who you are and what you do. I had a strong disability with tools. Pens and books were my world.

Choosing tasks for my son, which would show up my own inadequacies, is not something for the faint of heart. Yet vulnerability is essential in building that bond of trust between father and son. A son must see that his father is not afraid to try new things that he isn't good at.

Being a father means that you are doing more than just recreating another copy of yourself. A son should be given the chance to explore and experience a wide diversity of options available to men. And so we offered the task of building a tree fort. With just a hammer, a saw, some nails and whatever wood we could find. Remember the secret of the tasks is the character and confidence that is being built during the process.

The location for our tree fort was a seasoned wild olive tree in our back yard. Fifteen feet off the ground, the branches were splayed conveniently to set down a floor. Bracing and securing that floor required the agility of monkeys and the daring of a tiger. By setting up a ten-foot ladder and a few wooden foot braces on a tree branch we launched off on yet one more task.

Time: Fathers always seem to be busy with something. Setting apart time to help your son become a man often gets forgotten in the urgent requests of others. Not too many boys are begging their dads to set up 12 tasks that will stretch them and challenge them. Friends may be calling, entertainment and community events and school may be scheduling up time. It is easy to just let time slip by as the inconvenience of the tasks start to surface.

But here is where the character begins to develop. As the father commits himself to a journey with his son, there is an adjustment of attitude and action that emerges like a Monarch from a chrysalis. An adjustment, not just in the son, but in the father.

You begin to see your son through new eyes. You begin to assess the unique design that God wove together in the tapestry of strengths, skills, passions, challenges and dreams that make up your boy. It takes time, thought, and tenderness, but it is an investment which will yield returns far above any financial schemes calling for your heart.

The pastor leafed through the booklet again. "How about this one?" he said.

Pride: Anyone who knows me will know that I am immensely proud of my son. Michael has an inborn intensity which drives him. He is the firstborn of two firstborns and it shows.

My son's expectations for himself are high and his frustrations run deep when he falls short. It has always been this way. From even before the time he was a grade two boy trying to prove himself on the soccer field with the grade six boys. That year he read through the Chronicles of Narnia 7 times. He memorized a huge number of verses for

56

his Sunday School program. He explored his world like a pioneer possessed.

Choosing tasks for Michael wasn't just about finding something to keep him busy. Choosing tasks involved understanding his character strengths and weaknesses, his existing skill set and the gaps in that skill set, and it involved some awareness of the demands from the world in which he would take his place as a man. A father brings that overarching perspective of life, experience and understanding to help his son take some significant steps toward holistic interdependence in his world.

But even a father can only see so much. It is more important for the son to build a confidence that his father believes in him and will be there for him whenever possible. The details of the tasks are not as crucial as the heart connection that is happening in relationship along the way.

"Anything there that's helpful?" pastor Harris asked.

"Yes," Vincent said. "I think I might need to do this as much for my sake as for Stephen's. My dad had two tasks for my life. Carry on the family name and the family business."

"Wasn't there any hobby of his he tried to pass on to you?" the pastor asked.

"If you call the study of stars and herbal medicine a hobby," Vincent said. "I'm not sure I ever did either very well. I always seemed to just disappoint dad. There seemed to be no point to learning things from ancient times that no one needs anymore. We'll see you next week."

CHAPTER TEN

Wednesday brought the next surprise to Vincent. A phone message with Michael Harris as the caller sat on his desk among a pile of others which Jessica had left for him. He wondered how many Michael Harrises there could be so he called without certainty as to what he might be dealing with.

When he recognized Michael Harris's voice as the person he knew from the father-son group he assumed that the issue had to do with the 12 Tasks. When he found out that Michael was really looking for a new home, he felt even more uncertain as to which hat he should be wearing. He assured Michael of his ability to find what he was looking for and when the call was ended, he entered his search criteria into his computer and printed off the options that showed up.

Within an hour he called Michael back with five different options within the city limits and three just outside the boundaries. The next afternoon he took Michael on tour to see the three final choices.

A four-bedroom option in the Fraserview area of South Vancouver was the first stop. As Vincent and Michael stepped out of his BMW and moved toward the house Michael looked back at the nearby golf course. "Hard to beat this location. It'll be 8 blocks for high school when Matthew gets there, three blocks to the mall, and still within walking distance of the church."

Vincent added, "not to mention the golf course just down the block."

"If I could only golf," Michael said. "I should have had dad put that on my 12 Tasks."

Vincent stopped on the sidewalk and caught Michael's eye with a little hand wave. "Talking about the 12 Tasks, Michael. Did it really make all that much of a difference in your life? I mean, would you have turned out to be just the same kind of man you are now if you had just grown up in your family and in the circumstances you had?"

"That's a great question. I wonder that myself sometimes. I often look back at my journal and my 12 Tasks book and I'm amazed at the things I thought and the things I accomplished. I gained so much confidence and encouragement at a really important time of my life."

"What is this 12 Tasks book you're talking about?"

"The 12 Tasks book? That's a book my dad put together over the year I was doing all my tasks. It has pictures of me doing different tasks, it has letters and copies of the actual things I wrote and accomplished. It was the physical record and reminder of my step into manhood. Yes, physically I was still a boy at the end of the year but there was something different inside me when it was all over."

"Are you saying there's some kind of power in doing these 12 Tasks?"

"No. For me, the power of the 12 Tasks of Manhood was not as much in the specific tasks, but rather in the principles behind them, and the process I went through to accomplish them. It was the relevance for my life, the affirmation I gained, the impact on my identity, the relationship that was cemented, the flexibility of how things were set up, the trust that was shown in me."

"Can you give me examples?"

Michael moved to a nearby retaining wall on the property and sat down. Vincent joined him. "Well, when it comes to relevance, for example, my parents put a lot of thought into choosing tasks that were appropriate for me. I know my dad took the lead, but my mom was also involved along the way. Some tasks leveraged my strengths in writing, critical thinking, and relationship building. Other tasks helped to confront areas where I lacked confidence, such as my mechanical and athletic abilities. Together, the tasks attempted to build qualities like a strong work ethic, discipline, spiritual commitment, compassion for others, cultural understanding and leadership into my life. Seventeen years later I can even see more clearly how appropriate the tasks were."

"So, it's important to get this right from the start," Vincent said.

"It's important to know your son and to know the world in which he's living. You want to give him the best chance possible to succeed."

"Here, let me show you the yard while we talk," Vincent said. "This has a gorgeous garden which your wife will love. It's got good space for backyard barbecues for your small group. Enough privacy if you need it. It's even got a shed for all your handyman tools."

The realtor watched as Michael poked and prodded around the garage. "You were talking about the impact the tasks had on you. What did you mean by that?"

"Vincent, I guess I mean that my tasks were not just 'make work' projects," Michael said as he looked up and down the laneway. "It wasn't something done just to keep me busy and out of trouble. Each one was thoughtfully designed to have an intentional impact on my life. Reading through the Bible in a year helped provide a strong spiritual foundation for my transition to manhood and encouraged me to embrace my faith as my own. Building a tree fort gave me confidence that with hard work and dedication I could succeed where I was not naturally gifted. Writing a 70-page book solidified my love for the written word. My research article on the hardest part about growing up made me realize I was not alone in the challenges of teen life."

"Let me show you inside," Vincent said. "How did you feel affirmation through all this?"

"I believe affirmation is so important for a boy transitioning into manhood," Michael answered as the two men stepped into the kitchen. "I needed the security that my parents loved me unconditionally but they also recognized that I was growing up and were prepared to give me a much greater level of trust and responsibility. Affirmation had a huge role in the 12 Tasks." Michael continued opening cupboards, drawers and then the dish washer. "Not everything went smoothly and there were days I was unmotivated. My parent's encouragement and belief were huge. I will never forget the celebration we had upon completing the tasks. My parents invited adults who had influence in my life to speak words of encouragement and vision for the future. I wanted to be what they believed I could be."

"Let's look at the bedrooms," Vincent suggested. "What about the relationship issue you talked about? This is the part I really need to know about."

"It was something I needed to know as well," Michael said. "And it's something I'm counting on with Matthew when he goes through these tasks. The 12 Tasks deepened my relationship with my father. They provided a natural way for my Dad to relate with me that moved our relationship closer into the realm of mutual respect and friendship. The tasks we did together – like climbing Mount Kenya and building a tree fort were the most meaningful to me. I realized in the middle that there were areas where he felt just as incompetent as I did yet he still worked at it. These tasks have only become more meaningful to me in retrospect as I think about how to build a relationship with my own boys."

"This way to the basement," Vincent directed. "You and your dad have been talking about flexibility. How did that happen with the tasks?"

"My parents gave me some choice in the selection of tasks," Michael said. "They came up with 16 possible tasks and I was able to choose the 12 I wanted to accomplish. Perhaps even more important, they didn't see this list as completely sacrosanct and they ended up rewarding me with a bonus task during a time when they saw me standing up against prejudice. This was a quality they knew would be extremely important in my adult life and I still have the signed certificate from my father sharing why he was proud of me."

"That just about does it for this place," Vincent said. "The roof has just been replaced with a 50-year warranty on the new covering. New paint, new furnace, new energy star windows and appliances. One more question about the tasks."

"Shoot," Michael said. "I need to get Marlene over here to look at this. Now what do you need to know?"

"You mentioned trust," Vincent said. "Where did that fit into the whole program?"

"First, I don't think of the 12 Tasks as a program. It's more like a guided adventure through a transition with someone helping you." The two men stepped out on a front porch balcony to scan the neighborhood. Satisfied, Vincent locked up and marched down the stairs to the front walk. "The message I got from my parents, and especially my dad, was that I was being trusted. I can't understate the importance of this dynamic for a boy transitioning into manhood. The presence of trust as a boy grows older will greatly ease his transition. Its absence will be a considerable roadblock and will either lead to increasing animosity or unhealthy reliance. I will never forget a conversation I had with my Dad at age 16 when I had been deceitful about activities I was doing with my friends. He said he wanted to trust me and my actions were breaking down that trust. That short conversation was huge in my transition to manhood."

"So the tasks aren't the end of all this?" Vincent asked.

"They're the middle of a very important beginning," Michael said. "Now show me the other two houses. I need a good base for my son to do his 12 Tasks."

CHAPTER ELEVEN

It was ten pm on Friday night, while Vincent was looking at his emails, that he noticed an email from Michael. The message was entitled "thoughts."

He scanned the entry and noticed that there was an attachment. "Marlene likes the second place best but the price on the first one may suit our budget better. Let's keep talking. See attachment about my thoughts recorded several years ago on my climb with my dad. This is kind of my viewpoint regarding what he read to you when he felt like a failure."

Vincent opened the attachment and read.

Climbing Mount Kenya

I had to go on without him.

It was still pitch dark and freezing cold when our guide woke me up. My muscles ached as I scrambled out of my warm sleeping bag and pulled on layer after layer of clothing.

I was thirteen years old and our little group was sheltered in a rugged cabin located at 14,000 feet on Mount Kenya. Today was the day we made the final ascent to Point Lenana at just over 16,000 feet – the highest peak we could climb without technical equipment.

Climbing Mount Kenya was one of my twelve tasks. For the past two days my Dad and I had climbed with several other missionary parents who were facing the challenge together with their children. Dad had been sick for weeks leading up to the trip but still decided to go. I watched as he pushed his tired body step after step towards the peak. When I felt like quitting all I had to do was follow my Dad's example, and keep going.

But this morning, on the day of our ascent, he could barely lift his head from his pillow. This day it didn't matter how much willpower and strength he had. My Dad would not be climbing the final peak with me. I would be doing it for both of us.

The only picture I have left from the peak that day has me dressed in all red, with hands raised in victory alongside two other age-mates, as the sun rises over Point Lenana and the Batian peak behind it. At that moment the one person who was most responsible for my ascent lay flat on his back almost 2500 feet below me. And those two hands raised in victory were for both of us.

The transition to manhood has moments where the boy must continue the journey on his own, depending on his father's example and encouragement to reach the top."

Vincent could somehow feel the emotion of the moment when Michael raised his hands in victory for both he and his dad. He could also feel that sense of helplessness that Peter Harris might have felt as he lay in the bed below. He wanted to be there for his own son, Stephen, when the time counted and he knew that he had better start building a relationship that would result in a real victory for both of them.

The realtor heard Margaret rustling around in the kitchen

and called her in to read the email. When she finished reading, she sat down in the office chair opposite Vincent.

"Well," she said. "Does this mean you're committing yourself to this with Stephen?"

"I'd like to do what I can to feel like he can be at the top celebrating one day," Vincent said.

"This would be a good time for you to use your persuasive powers. Stephen had a talk with me today and said he was having doubts about whether he could do this or not. He was working on some list about growth areas and said he had too many weaknesses compared to all the other boys. He really doubts that he can do this."

Vincent stood up and began pacing in the small space by his desk. "I'm the one who's been having doubts about whether I could do this or not. Maybe he's picking up vibes from my own lack of self-confidence and thinking that I don't think he can make it either."

"I think you need to be vulnerable with your son right now," Margaret said. "The only thing he hears from you is about you being the number one real estate agent. I think this is a good time to let him know that maybe you're human after all."

Vincent found Stephen in his own bedroom reading a sci-fi novel and he stood in the door waiting for acknowledgement. When nothing happened, he stepped into the room. "Permission to come aboard," he said.

"Permission granted," Stephen muttered. "Why do you have to be so lame? Why don't you just talk to me like other dads?"

Vincent pulled up a chair and sat down a few feet from the

bed. "I guess I have to admit that I don't know how other dads talk to their sons. I've had years of practice but I still feel like I'm kind of new at this."

"Fine," Stephen said. "Did mom tell you I don't want to go tomorrow?"

"She told me that you were having doubts about whether you could grow in every area all at once," Vincent said. "I told her I thought I was the one having all the doubts about whether I could do this?"

"What do you have to worry about?" Stephen asked. "I'm the one who has to do the tasks to become a man?"

"I guess I was seeing this a little differently," Vincent said. "I thought I was supposed to show you what a man was and help you do what you had to do in order to become what you were already designed to be. I was feeling like maybe I wasn't man enough to do that for you."

"I'm not sure what you were just trying to say," Stephen said, "but if you're trying to say you're feeling the same as me then I doubt it."

"I just want to know if you'll do one thing," Vincent said.

"What's that?"

"Will you go with me tomorrow and just see what we think after the session is done? Maybe everyone else is feeling the same as we are. Maybe this isn't as hard as we're making it out to be."

"Fine. But Dad, can you narrow my growth areas down to just four or five so I have a chance?"

"Done!"

For some reason Saturday felt like a different experience

for Vincent as he and Stephen arrived at the Harris home. Everyone was there except for Samuel Ortiz and his son Jimmy.

"I'm afraid that the Ortiz's felt like they wouldn't be able to participate in the 12 Tasks," pastor Harris said. "This might be more demanding than you feel you can handle. My son and I are only giving you a tool to use if you would like it. Feel free to take it, modify it, or drop out at any time. There is no pressure from us. If you can find a better way to help your son become a man, please use it. This is just something that worked really well for us and others we know. We believe that a real wisdom and courage and strength can come from doing these 12 Tasks together. I have a wedding I need to perform so Michael will take care of things today. I have great confidence that by being here those of you who are fathers are making a statement of confidence in your sons. And I believe you boys are showing great trust in your fathers. Both of you will not regret this."

No one else had any input so Michael gave his son Matthew some sheets of paper to hand out to all the survivors who were still in the room. "This was put together by my dad," Michael said, after pastor Harris walked out.

Vincent took his sheet and read over it as he'd been instructed to.

The twelve tasks encourage a father to see his son's ability (as designed by God), to provide initial opportunity, and to foster motivation. It isn't helpful to create tasks beyond genuine ability, or to select tasks where no opportunity will exist, or to design a series of challenges without sufficient motivation.

A father's modeled example before his son, significant participation beside his son, and consistent gentle coaching behind his son, will provide the stimulus to keep from getting discouraged and give up.

There is no way that I could expect Michael to be a top ranked mechanic, engineer, or carpenter when I never modeled those abilities, never exposed him to opportunities to learn, and never gave him motivation to acquire the skills needed. Perhaps, in a different environment, I should have. Instead, he learned to communicate passionately with people about significant human tragedy through verbal and written mediums.

My expectations are buffered by what I modeled, gave opportunity for, and motivated him toward. They are also channeled by the community and environment we live in, the other models in my son's relational sphere, and the buy-in from other family members.

Michael's tasks encouraged him to see the peak and to take a step toward it. He still does that. His tasks encouraged him to express himself, to understand his world, and to engage with it. He still does that. The twelve tasks challenged his mind, his body, and his soul.

The tasks are not just jobs to complete and check off. They are character builders designed to stimulate what is happening inside the son so that he has all he needs when his body grows, his opportunities expand, and his relationships and environment shift around him.

TASK	ABILITY 1-5	OPPORTUNITY 1-5	MOTIVATION 1-5	TOTAL
1.				
2.				
3.				
4.				
5.				
6.				
7.				

Charting your son's potential tasks might help give you an overview of what you want to focus on. As you dream, list the task. Set a numerical equivalent to show his ability, opportunity or motivation for this task. Set the number together - father and son (and mother).

Ability is not about how much your son is already involved in this type of activity, but rather how much you see he is able to grow in this area. Opportunity is about whether there is a serious chance of doing this task. [ie. Setting the task to climb Mt. Kenya would be unrealistic if you lived on the prairies and had few resources to travel to where the task could be done.] Motivation is about how well this task syncs with your son's internal dreams, desires and willingness to face personal risks and challenges.

Hopefully, you haven't waited until your son's pre-teens to begin modeling and motivating him toward manhood.

"So, let me get this straight," Njoroge said when he was done reading. "You want us to limit what we're asking our sons to do to just 12 things that involve opportunity, ability and motivation. And I'm assuming you don't mean video games, Facebook and iPods."

Njoroge put his arm around his son and the two-fist bumped and gently knocked the sides of their heads together.

"I just want you to work together with your son to find 12 challenges that will build the character of a man into your son," Michael said. "What I would suggest from my own experience is that you actually try to come up with sixteen or more and then narrow it down."

The rest of the afternoon was spent filling out the chart and brainstorming on two major tasks that the whole group could do together. The time had finished and the choices for group tasks had been narrowed down to four. A canoe and camping trip, a mountain climb, a weekend serving at a rescue mission, and a barbecue for the community hosted by the fathers and sons. The group was to stay in email contact and try to narrow down the choices to two by the following weekend.

When Vincent left, he had no doubt that he and Stephen were committed to the 12 Tasks. He wasn't sure he had a whole lot more confidence in himself but he could see that his son had a lot more hope to try whatever lay ahead.

CHAPTER TWELVE

Tuesday, the pressure at the office tripled. Tuesday, the room temperature shot up. Tuesday, Shepherd returned.

Jessica alerted Vincent first by walking into his doorway and using her thumb to warn him about the upcoming confrontation. With Rick away, he should have been able to make up more ground but he was still only third in sales.

If only he had pressured Michael and Marlene a little more for a commitment. Or if he had spent more time working his phone instead of working on the 12 Tasks with Stephen. He was still putting in 12-hour days but it never seemed to be enough when the major marketing was overseas.

Shepherd's first words were meant to be as caustic as they sounded. "Lau, do you think we're running a charity here? We just dropped to second on the overall Asian marketing. What were you doing while I was away drumming up business?"

There were no words that would help so Vincent stood quietly and waited for the verbal tirade to finish. Shepherd called over his shoulder as he walked out again. "I'm thinking that I'll be seeing Rick's name on your door by this time next week. If you're religious, this is a good time to start praying to anyone who's listening."

Vincent slumped down on his chair and looked at the Woodrow Wilson quote on the card that Michael had given him. "No man has ever risen to the real stature of spiritual manhood until he has found that it is finer to serve somebody else than it is to serve himself."

'Was he only serving himself with this job?' He didn't know how else to improve his output without sacrificing his family and himself. The thought of calling Peter Harris dropped into his consciousness and he instinctively dialed the church number. Amber, the secretary, put him through to the pastor.

"I need a minute with a mentor," Vincent said after greetings were exchanged. "I need to make some big decisions."

"What's on your mind?" pastor Harris asked.

"I'm under a lot of pressure at work," Vincent said. "I used to love selling real estate but the time and energy I need to keep up with the demands is impacting my marriage and my parenting. I'm not sure what's important anymore. The 12 Tasks sound like they could be really important for my son and even for our relationship but I'm not sure how to both be there for him and keep my job and marriage as well."

"Sounds like we should talk a little more about this," pastor Harris said. "There are a lot of us fathers who face that same balancing act."

The pastor was booked up for the next few days so Vincent made an appointment for the following Tuesday afternoon. He hoped he still had a job by then.

By some mercy, he managed to avoid Shepherd the rest of the week and he actually managed to make enough sales to feel a sense of satisfaction with his performance. Perhaps his silent prayers were being heard after all.

On Saturday, the father-son event started with a brainstorm about the different kinds of categories which could be the focus of a task. When they were done Michael read off the list. "Spiritual, personal, financial, physical, sexual, moral, ethical, global, relational, social, verbal, character, biblical, mechanical, musical, creative, literary, intuitive, compassion, teachable," he read. "That's twenty different areas to consider. Other things you might consider include whether your son is an extrovert or an introvert, whether he enjoys the outdoors or indoors, whether he is more feeling oriented or thinking oriented."

"How in the world are we supposed to narrow this down?" Hanny Prakash asked. "This is looking way more complicated than just coming up with 12 Tasks."

"Good question," Michael said. "Some of you know your sons already very well and coming up with tasks may be really straightforward. I just want to offer you another tool in case you get stuck along the way. The chart that Matthew will be handing to you is just to help encourage you to put some thought into the tasks that you'll be choosing. It will help you identify strengths and growth areas."

"I thought we'd already chosen the strengths and growth areas we were going to work on," said Navid. "What do we do with the lists we've already made up?"

"Another good question," Michael said. "This chart is just to help you confirm what you think and to help clarify what we mean by each area of consideration. The five questions will assist you in identifying potential tasks you might want to include. I'm just trying to keep you thinking as broadly as possible. I have copies of the full list of categories and questions if anyone wants to see me later."

"Why didn't we get this earlier?" Hanny asked. "It might

have made it easier to get this before we had to choose the tasks instead of after? Isn't this a bit backwards?"

"My apologies," Michael said. "I just sat down this week and put this together in case you needed it. Some of you seemed to be having trouble narrowing things down. You don't have to use it if you've already got your work done. This isn't a course we're taking. We're just dads trying to help each other raise our sons."

Vincent accepted his sheet from Matthew and then voiced the question that was erupting in the back of his mind. "What were the results of the two tasks we were supposed to choose over this past week? What are we going to do together?'

"Sure, let's handle that now and you can all take this sheet home and look at it," Michael said. "We actually had a tie for the main tasks – you chose to take a camping canoe trip and to hike up a mountain as your preference but so many of you made comments about wanting to be involved in the street ministry that I have a suggestion."

"What's the suggestion?" Njoroge asked.

"I'm suggesting that we take one night to do a trial task just to see how we work as father and son teams. I have contacts at Potter's Mission on the east side," Michael said, "and they're willing to let us come down tonight for a few hours to help in their soup kitchen."

Jesse Browning spoke up. "I've got family commitments tonight but I'm fine if everyone else wants to go. I just need to make sure we've got some solid dates for our canoe trip so I can book holidays."

The discussion lasted twenty minutes around the choices

before the majority of the group decided to break early this day and reconvene at five to take public transit down to the Potter's Mission.

CHAPTER THIRTEEN

That evening, Vincent was proud of Stephen as he watched his son first chop vegetables and then serve the men and women of the streets. On the way into the soup kitchen Vincent had noticed the dozens of scantily dressed prostitutes and the bedraggled addicts actually shooting up on the streets. One woman was injecting directly into a vein in her neck. He was tempted to grab his son and run home but he stayed to be with the group.

Vincent was scrubbing out a soup pot when he noticed that Stephen was nowhere in the kitchen with the others. He felt the surge of anger and embarrassment that his son was avoiding work and then he felt the concern and anxiety that perhaps something terrible had happened to Stephen.

The realtor grabbed a towel and made his way out of the kitchen. Stephen was sitting close to a frail, middle-aged man with tattered clothing and stringy brown hair. They were engaged in intense conversation and Stephen was leaning in so he didn't miss a word.

Vincent made his way through the dozens of individuals who still lingered at the tables. Some were nursing a cup of coffee or cocoa and some were just carrying on conversations with others who sat near them. As he neared his son, he heard the voice of the street person he was listening to.

"Well, first, I lost my only son, Tommy," the man said. "Then I lost his mom, 'cause she was so broken hearted at losing her boy. She just got up and left. I was so depressed over losing my family that I couldn't focus at work and I lost my job. Then I couldn't make my mortgage payments and I lost my house. Once you get caught on the streets it is so hard to get out of here. That's why I'm thankful to God for people like you who take time to notice someone like me. I didn't want to be here. It just kind of happened."

Vincent was stunned when he heard his son offer to pray with the man. As far as he knew, Stephen had never been to this area of town. Neither had he seen poverty firsthand before. How had his son learned to do this? Vincent knew he, himself, would have walked right past the man if he'd seen him on the street.

Stephen raised his head after praying, saw his dad, and actually smiled. "This is Frank, Dad," he said. "Frank, this is my dad."

Frank turned and put out his hand. "I'm pleased to meet the father of such a fine young man," he said. "You ought to be very proud of this boy. He's going to go places. You keep him off the streets, you hear? A fine young man like this needs to know his daddy loves him and is there for him. I'll be going now but thanks for the dinner and the prayers. God listens to good boys like you so keep it up. And keep remembering me. The name's Frank. I once had a boy just like you. Right good boy he was. God bless you with all the best blessings. Bye, now."

Vincent watched the man hobble out of the door along with others who were finding their places for the night. The team finished cleaning up and then headed out on the streets to find a bus. Stephen wanted to talk to the mission director a little more so Vincent assured the others that they would be along in a short time and to go ahead.

A block from the mission Vincent heard a loud "hey," from Stephen. Stephen had been walking right behind him in the crowded area. "My iPod!" Stephen yelled. "He stole my iPod."

Vincent looked around at the milling crowd of bodies in the gathering darkness. Stephen was moving away from him after the thief. "Wait," he called but Stephen was intent on only one thing. Getting back his iPod.

Bodies seemed to be standing in Vincent's way and he felt like a salmon fighting through intense rapids to make any headway. "Stephen! Stephen!" Vincent hollered. "Stephen, come back."

As Vincent reached a street corner the light turned red for his crossing. He was about to step out when the blare of a car horn startled him as a driver turned right around the corner in front of him. He stepped back and looked hard for his son. He refused to look back at the others gathering at the corner.

The anxious father thought he caught a glimpse of Stephen rushing into an alley half a block away. While others ambled across the road, between the cars swishing their way slowly along the puddled surface of the street, Vincent couldn't force himself to break the law and try again.

The agony inside tore him apart as the seconds passed and others continued to ignore the red light. Finally, he saw the amber light showing and rushed across toward the alley. The darkness of the lane swallowed him up, much like the whale had swallowed Jonah, and he slowed his sprint to a walk.

As his eyes adjusted, he stepped forward with all senses alert. He could hear moans coming from alcoves and behind dumpsters along the route but nothing sounded like Stephen.

At the end of the alley Vincent noticed a crowd growing in a parking lot. He immediately thought the worst as he raced over.

It seemed like an eternity treading through the dozens of bodies, but suddenly Stephen was standing in front of him with a smiling Frank by his side. "Frank did it," said Stephen with exuberance. "Frank tackled the thief and got my iPod back. He was amazing. I'm going to give him the iPod, Dad, okay?"

"It's yours," Vincent said. "But remember, if you give it away, you'll have to earn the money to get another one."

"That's okay," Stephen said. "Frank needs it more than I do. I've got some really great tunes on here and he needs the encouragement. You and I have each other but he's got no one. Maybe this will remind him that God is going to take care of him. Dad, we've got to come back and do this again."

On the way home, Vincent kept glancing over at the son seated next to him. The son who kept his eye on the streets. The son who kept smiling in a way the realtor hadn't seen in years. Maybe there was something to this task business.

CHAPTER FOURTEEN

It was late Thursday night before Vincent had a chance to look at the latest sheet from Michael. He'd been blitzed with calls and offers seemingly through very little effort of his own. It was amazing how world markets, government legislation and local economics impacted housing costs.

He was surprised by the number of first-time local buyers since his specialty was the Asian market. Michael and Marlene still hadn't committed and he was having a hard time from competitive bids that were coming in on the place they wanted.

Stephen seemed to have improved in his math marks thanks to Navid's patient tutoring. He also seemed to be more upbeat about the possibility of the 12 Tasks with his birthday coming up in 2 weeks.

The father and son had talked through some options in line with Stephen's strengths. They had talked about the possibility of a sports option where Stephen could join the church Ultimate team or else a community club soccer team he'd been thinking about. It seemed a bit difficult to establish personal goals which involved a team sport and a coach's discretion about playing time.

They had talked through options involving the writing of a short book on the challenges of being a teenager in today's world but Stephen wasn't sure his skills were good enough. They had talked about training to run a marathon but thought that might be too challenging – especially if Victor had to be involved.

Victor thought they should take a course on woodworking at night school but Stephen wasn't sure he wanted to go to school all day and then again at night. Stephen suggested something to do with helping out at the street mission or at the transition homes for refugees set up by the church. Perhaps they could put on a community dinner.

Vincent suggested that Stephen read through the Bible and memorize one of the gospels. Stephen suggested that perhaps he could memorize a smaller book like James or Philippians.

Stephen suggested that he might be interested in putting together a video documentary on the life of street people and this one project began to excite both of them as they dreamed through what needed to happen.

The jumble of potential tasks, and especially the video documentary, wormed its way through Vincent's mind as he picked up the sheet from Michael.

The categories discussed were clearly the same ones the men had brainstormed last Saturday but the questions attached to them provided a little more insight into what was involved in each area. Vincent put his mind to digesting the samples which Michael had given. The first page seemed to be more instructions.

The following pages contained the specifics he was looking for.

Statements: check off the level which is true for your son. Four or five statements in the same category at level 3 or 4 would indicate a strength for your son. This is an important time for honest reflection and perhaps conversation with your son. If you think of a phrase that better captures the essence of your son in one particular area, and you know this would help you formulate a task for your son, feel free to substitute your phrase for one of the ones listed. Or add it if that works better. This is a guideline to help you.

1 = Never True 2 = Occasionally True 3 = Usually True 4 = Always True

Spiritual:

	1.	2.	3.	4.
a.				
b.				
c.				
d.				
e.				

a. My son prays freely and comfortably (alone, in a group)

b. My son loves to read his Bible

c. My son studies and memorizes Scripture

d. My son adjusts his life to what he reads in the Bible

e. My son is a positive influence on his peers

Personal:

	1.	2.	3.	4.
a.				
b.				
c.				
d.				
e.				

a. My son treats others with dignity and respect

b. My son practices self-control consistently

c. My son thinks through consequences for his actions

d. My son is worthy of trust and is respected by adults

e. My son is respectful of and considerate toward authority

Financial:

	1.	2.	3.	4.
a.				
b.				
c.				
d.				
e.				

a. My son knows how to save his money wisely

b. My son understands the importance of tithing

c. My son is ready to earn his money with good work

d. My son spends his money wisely

e. My son is learning to be generous with others

Physical:

	1.	2.	3.	4.
a.				
b.				
c.				
d.				
e.				

a. My son lives an active lifestyle on a regular basis

b. My son has learned to value healthy eating

c. My son gets a good balance of sleep and exercise

d. My son refrains from engaging in senseless risky behavior

e. My son is not afraid to be challenged physically

Sexual:

	1.	2.	3.	4.
a.				
b.				
c.				
d.				
e.				

a. My son treats his own body with dignity and respect
b. My son practices self-control consistently
c. My son thinks through consequences for his actions
d. My son is worthy of trust and is respected by adults
e. My son speaks respectfully about women and girls

There were five statements of evaluation for each of the twenty categories the men had designated.

The main thing that hit Vincent was how many gaps there were in his awareness about Stephen. He decided that the next several weeks would have to focus on investing in building a stronger relationship with his son.

Later that evening he made an intentional effort to leave his computer and to crawl up onto the bed as Margaret prepared for her night time novel read.

"Now this is a surprise," his wife said. "I'm sure we just had our date night two days ago. Must have been a really good one to get you out of the woods so soon."

Vincent saw the smirk on her face and the glint in her eye and was glad to have his wife feeling a little more relaxed again. "I'd take five date nights a week if we could work it out," he teased back. "Move on over. I've got something to show you."

Margaret listened as Vincent tried to explain a little more about the purpose of the chart and about the types of tasks that he and Stephen were discussing. It was clear from the ensuing discussion that this mother knew her son. She also understood how the chart could be used to help bring focus to the exercise.

Vincent left the bed feeling like he'd done something special in sharing the journey a little more with his wife. He'd been carrying a lot of the pressure for his son's outcome and he realized that Margaret would still be a key player in the year ahead.

Now he understood that the charts were tools to help him if he needed it and not grade school tests to pass or fail on. He could feel his breathing coming easier the next time he sat down with Stephen to narrow down the options.

CHAPTER FIFTEEN

Vincent knew he was holding his own when he was still in his same office three weeks after Shepherd's threat. Jessica was working her hardest to support him in making and following up on contacts and he felt a strong pull to stay longer hours out of gratitude for her efforts.

By the time Stephen's birthday had come and gone three of the father-son teams had launched their 12 Tasks and Vincent and Stephen had finalized their list and set out a timeline for the first two.

The next task involved a series of running events that would cumulate in 200 miles total racing. The Sun Run was a short introduction and Vincent had actually enjoyed the few times he and Stephen had gone out jogging and training for the event. Stephen seemed to be running several times a week but Vincent saved his running for Sunday afternoons because of work.

It was the Friday afternoon before the race, just as Vincent was dumping his last files back on Jessica's desk, that Shepherd stopped by. "I'll need you this weekend both Saturday and Sunday."

"Can't do it," Vincent said. "I'm in the Sun Run with Stephen. I'm already committed."

"Well, you better uncommit yourself," Shepherd said. "We've got a dozen of your Hong Kong contacts who are coming in tonight for two days of viewing. The specs will be here in an hour and I want to give them more than they can handle so they'll be back for more. These are key players who can open up the floodgates to more of those mainland millionaires over there."

"I really don't think I can do this."

"Rick wants this bad," Shepherd said, "but I told him they were your contacts first. The bonus from this will go a long way to help with that mortgage of yours and it'll guarantee you hanging onto this office for a few more months. This isn't an option. Make it happen."

Jessica gave Vincent a sorrowful look as Shepherd disappeared down the hall. "I'll stay if you need me. I can cover all the paperwork while you're running around."

"I'd appreciate that," Vincent said. "I better call Margaret and Stephen. I don't know how I'm going to explain this one to my son."

Vincent felt trapped and angry. He felt even worse after his conversation with Margaret.

Before calling Stephen, he decided to call Njoroge since he and his son Toby were also going on the Sun Run.

Njoroge picked up the call in the way that only Njoroge could get away with. "Hey, Hong Kong running man, you all ready for heart attack alley? The Sun Run is the Fun Run."

"That's what I'm calling you about," Vincent said. "My boss just walked in and told me we have clients coming in from Hong Kong. I have to be with them all weekend."

"Ouch!" Njoroge said. "What have you told Stephen?"

"I haven't called him yet," Vincent admitted. "I wanted to talk with you first to see what my options might be."

"Well, send him with Toby and me," Njoroge said. "We're still running and there's no reason he can't come with us. It's like when pastor Harris couldn't get up that mountain and some of the other fathers had to take Michael to the top. I'll make sure he's running in victory for both of you."

"Hey, I'd really appreciate that," Vincent said. "Maybe I can make it up to you on one of the other tasks."

"Hakuna Matata, Houseman!" Njoroge said. "If one of our tasks involves selling houses, you'll be first on my list to call."

He managed to reach Stephen on his way home from Alejandro's. The distraught father did his best to explain the unexpected situation to his disappointed son and how Maxwell and Toby Njoroge would be still running with him in the Sun Run. To Vincent's surprise Stephen took the news quite well and even accepted the offered apology with grace. He wondered if something was changing between them.

Jessica booked a room for Vincent in the hotel next door to the office so he wouldn't have to commute home over the weekend. She even took a run to his place to retrieve an extra suit and a packed bag that Margaret had put together for him. She seemed to anticipate his every need even before he asked.

Vincent enjoyed the quick interactions as they exchanged needs and thoughts for the coming weekend. It was past midnight on Friday before he even realized the time that had passed.

When Vincent finally grabbed his suit jacket and brief case, he was pleasantly surprised to see Jessica standing at the elevator as she left. When they reached the ground floor she kept up with him stride for stride continuing the pleasant banter about how they were going to work as a team to take back first place. When she followed him into the hotel lobby next door he hesitated.

"I'm sure I can find my room," he said. "You've looked after me enough today."

"I'm sure you can find your room as well," she said. "It's right next to mine. If you think I'm spending the weekend in a taxi you're wrong. I'm going to be available every minute you need me."

Vincent wasn't sure how to respond but decided to take this as professionally as possible. The two of them signed into their own rooms, got their own keys, rode the elevator together and said good-nights as they went into their separate rooms. And that was that.

After a good shower in the morning Vincent was happy to see Jessica already at the hotel breakfast bar. A cup of coffee was already sitting at the place opposite her and he sat down without questioning. As usual, it was prepared just the way he liked it. She'd even selected some of his favourite pastries.

Saturday was a blur of activity as Vincent spent ten hours selling the city and some of its higher end housing. Two extended white limousines had been hired for the event and the group covered the North, South, and West sides of the city. For dinner that evening they took a gondola ride up Grouse Mountain and watched the sun set over the harbour and bustling metropolis below them.

After dropping off the Hong Kong investors at ten pm, Vincent headed back to his hotel. Jessica was waiting in the lobby for his latest report. They'd been in touch off and on during the day to make sure all was running smooth but the adrenaline was high for both of them and they weren't ready for sleep.

Without words, they turned into the café that was still open and ordered coffees. The details of the day flowed easily from Vincent and Jessica encouraged him with the successes he was forseeing. It was one am as they reached the elevators. When they stepped into the elevators Jessica stood behind him. She put her hands gently on his shoulders and massaged lightly.

"You really need to relax," she said.

Vincent's first thought oddly was about Stephen. His son was running the Sun Run in the morning without him. His son was running for both of them. He was not going to do anything to disappoint his son any further.

He waited patiently for the elevator to reach their floor and then turned to Jessica. "I can't tell you how much I appreciate what you've done for me this weekend," he said. "I think the thing that will help me relax the most is to get a good sleep. I know you want to live your life without regrets just as much as I do. When your future husband comes looking for references, I want to give you the highest one possible. Thank you for going far beyond the call of duty to make this weekend work. We've got one more day. Let's finish well. Have a good sleep."

He refused to look back as he entered the code and opened his door. Being a man involved a lot more than just passing 12 Tasks. He knew that his roles as husband and father and boss required all the wisdom he could gain.

Although he didn't sleep that well through the night his soul was at peace. When he came down for breakfast there was no sign of Jessica. He drank his coffee alone and tried to figure out what other details needed to be done.

As he was preparing to leave, Jessica stepped out of the elevator. She was dressed in a sea blue blouse and white capris.

The most casual outfit he had ever seen her in. She didn't hesitate to drop off her key at the desk and then walk to his side with a smile.

"Well boss. We've got a busy day ahead. Thanks to you I woke up with no regrets and I'm going to be expecting a pretty good reference for that future husband of mine."

"You got it," Vincent said.

"I hope your wife realizes what a good man she married."

"I hope so too. Jessica, if you can give me a minute, I just need to call my son to encourage him for his race today."

CHAPTER SIXTEEN

Vincent and Stephen sat side by side on the couch watching an old video clip of Nik Wallenda walking the tight rope across Niagara Falls. The seventh generation dare devil was the first to accomplish the feat from Buffalo, New York to Niagara Falls, Ontario. Every step seemed a prayer until he ran the last few steps and landed safely. Up to a billion people had watched and cheered the courage of one man who was determined to do the impossible.

"Now that's a task I'm glad we didn't put on my list," Stephen said.

"Did you see Nik's dad talking him through that walk?" Vincent asked. "I would not have wanted to be on the end of that headset if anything went wrong."

"Don't worry dad," Stephen said. "I'm not going to put you into a place where you're going to regret it. All we have is the canoe and mountain trip next week and then three more tasks. I think we've done pretty good so far."

"You know," Vincent said. "I've decided something after watching you head down to Potter's mission every Friday for the last three months. If you keep that up for another month, I'm going to write you a certificate which will let you substitute that accomplishment for any of the three tasks you haven't done yet. I'm calling it the Heart of Compassion Award."

"Wow, thanks dad," Stephen said. "I actually love going down there. It doesn't seem like a task. It's been good to see Frank getting back on his feet again. He's almost adopted me the way he carries on. I think he just needed a reason to try again. He told me that some day I'm going to see him in church."

Vincent lightly elbowed Stephen in the ribs. "Just don't forget your real dad, son."

Stephen stepped away and then reached out for a fist bump. "Don't worry, dad. After this year, I could never forget."

"Okay, bud. We've got to make sure we've got all our gear together for that canoe trip. I'm proud of the way you pulled through in school this year and I know I'll be proud of the way you finish this big task. Have you got the list that the group put together?"

"Yeah," Stephen said. "Toby, Darius, Matthew, Seth and I divided up who was going to bring what. We're thinking the dads are going to have to carry some significant weight if we're going to bring everything we need. We're limiting ourselves to 50 pounds each although Darius says he can do 70."

"Let's double-check things and see if there's anything we can leave behind," Vincent said. "This is a survival trip, not a holiday resort. We're living off the land as much as possible for one whole week. You've done great research on the equipment we need and the route we're going to take. Let's get to it."

The last week of preparation involved two team meetings where the supplies were collected and reconsidered until the absolute essentials were chosen. Packs were put together in line with what each father or son could carry and then a few luxury items were added where space permitted. As much as possible the boys were given the responsibilities of planning and organizing with coaching from the fathers.

The first three days would involve a canoe trip so extra supplies could be stowed in the canoes. It was the three-day mountain climb that would test the strength of each of them with their packs. Five fathers and five sons had committed themselves to making this task the mark of manhood. Vincent spent Thursday evening wondering if he was getting in over his head. Walking a wire cable over Niagara Falls suddenly seemed more doable than what he saw facing him and Stephen.

He kissed Margaret good-bye on Friday at lunch and asked for her prayers. He tried to impress the image of her smile and last wave on his mind as he set out for his wilderness adventure. They met the others in the church parking lot and loaded up a van for the ten of them.

Michael Harris was there with his son Matthew. Navid Samadi was there with Darius. Maxwell Njoroge was there with Toby. And Hanny Prakash was there with Jimmy. It was a good crew.

The soft white clouds floating across the sky gave a peaceful sense to the eager adventurers below. The sun felt warm on their bare arms. Everything appeared to be in order for the boys to become men and the men to become boys.

"Who checked the weather reports?" Hanny asked.

"Sunny with cloudy periods mixed with cloud and sunny periods," Njoroge said with a wide smile. "It's summer. The sun won't melt us and the rain won't shrink us. We're good to go."

"Okay," Michael said. "Last equipment check. Haul out your gear and let's make sure we have what we need. I'll read the list. If you have it just yell check."

When the fathers and sons had pulled everything out into the parking lot the list was read.

"1. A good solid backpack with water bottles."

"Check!" called out the group.

"2. A well-ventilated tent with places to store things inside."

"Check!"

"It would make things lighter if we slept under the stars," Njoroge piped in.

"3. A light Coleman camping stove for cooking with fuel."

"Check!"

"It would also make it lighter if we cooked over an open fire," Hanny joked.

"4. A goose down sleeping bag."

"Check!"

"Hey, that reminds me," broke in Navid. "How do you get down off an elephant? Don't know? You don't. You get down off a duck. Get it?"

"5. A Therma rest sleeping pad."

"Check!"

"What are we setting up?" Vincent asked. "A hotel?"

"6. Dishes and food items as we designated for each of you."

"Check!"

"Who brought the T-bone steaks?" Hanny chirped.

"7. Coffee and tea and hot chocolate."

"Check!"

"First one up makes the coffee," Njoroge said.

"8. Good shoes and hiking poles for the fathers."

"Check!"

"9. Rain jacket, poncho, plastic to cover your tent."

"Check!"

"10. Multi-blade knife and bear spray."

"Check!"

"Are we allowed to pat the grizzlies?" Jimmy Prakash asked in jest.

"It's starting to feel like we're checking out a plane for take-off," added his father, Hanny.

"11. Extra light weight sweat shirts or hoodies."

"Check!"

"12. Flashlight with extra batteries."

"Check!"

"13. First Aid Kit and Matches and Firestarter kit."

"Check!"

"14. Can opener."

"Check!"

"15. Hat and gloves and a pillow case."

"Check!"

"16. Whistle and Thermometer."

"Check!"

"17. Freezer bags."

"Check!"

"Freezer bags?" Hanny mocked. "You expecting us to do this trip cold turkey? Get it? Freezer bags - Cold Turkey?"

"18. Extra carabineers."

"Check!"

"19. Rope for a clothesline."

"Check!"

"20. Gatorade and trail mix."

"Check!"

"21. Toiletries and a shovel."

"Check!"

"22. Bug spray, duck tape, pot scrubber, sunscreen, ground tarp, sewing kit."

"Check!"

"Did I forget anything?" Michael asked.

"Yeah, what about a GPS or a compass?" Darius asked.

"We brought a map," Michael said. "Hopefully, none of us are planning on getting lost."

"Do they have Wi-Fi or should I leave my laptop at home?" Hanny joked.

"Let's just get this stuff loaded up and get there before dark," Vincent said. "We've got five hours to the entrance gate at the provincial park and we need to beat rush hour traffic. I'm just glad our first night is in a cabin. Our canoes are supposed to be in the water at 7 am."

CHAPTER SEVENTEEN

The trip to the provincial park was uneventful. The boys endured the manufactured humor and banter of their fathers without too much comment. The fathers resurrected stories from past adventures and expanded them to fit the occasion. The ice was gradually being broken between generations.

The group was split into two cabins and the Laus were matched with the Harrises and the Prakashes. After hot chocolate and a time around a campfire, roasting marshmallows, the group settled in for a time of chatter from their sleeping bags. One by one the voices stilled until only the bullfrogs and crickets were heard in the night.

Before 6 am Michael Harris was prodding the others to get up and engage the day. A quick meal of toast and eggs and Canadian back bacon energized the team to haul the equipment to the waiting canoes. Two guides, Marshall and Andeep, met them at the edge of the water.

There would be one canoe for each father and son pair. Instructions for loading were given and when that was successfully accomplished Marshall and Andeep proceeded to give a short course on handling a canoe. Bright yellow life jackets were handed out and put on.

Vincent stood looking out at the scene. The water was like a mirror reflecting the majesty of snow-capped mountains, lush forests, and cloud studded skies. A pair of eagles were rising on thermals across the lake and for as long as he listened there wasn't one cell phone ringing, one car honking, or one boss yelling.

The realtor also noticed the strong domination of the Douglas fir trees along the lake front and foothills all around. There were patches of cottonwood and aspen in some areas. Higher up he could see the Lodgepole pines and the spruce trees. Nearing the hill tops he could see fir trees and balsam and a few species he couldn't identify.

Birdsong was everywhere like a mighty orchestra designed to call forth the day. The chatter of ground squirrels caught the realtor's attention. The water pulled at his heart like a magnet to a pin and he took the initiative to step aboard and grab his paddle.

The others followed his lead and soon the fathers and sons were trailing in the subtle wake of Marshall and Andeep as they stroked their way across the lake. Nothing could be better than this.

Just after ten, the lead canoes pulled up to an island camp so that the men could refresh themselves, stretch and do whatever else was necessary. The waters of this azure lake again mirrored the jagged peaks and rich forest all around.

Andeep and Marshall handed out fishing poles to the group and it wasn't long before a dozen plump trout had been pulled from the waters. The guides gave a basic course on gutting, filleting and preparing the fish for eating. Each boy was called on to take care of his own share of the catch and before noon the smell of frying trout started the saliva working in the mouths of both fathers and sons.

Vincent spent extra time washing up, trying to get the smell of the fish off of his hands, and Stephen teased him about wearing gloves next time. The father and son were already sensing a transition in their relationship.

Andeep stood up to address the group. "Lesson one: Don't take more than you need. Lesson two: leave the place you've been as if you've never been there. We're back in the water in 30. Let's do it."

Vincent and Stephen watched the two guides carefully as they disposed of fish guts, replaced rods in the cabin, and packed up the canoes again. A final scan was made of the area for trash, a thumbs up from the guides, and the journey was underway again. In the next few hours they traversed two more small lakes and a significant section of river.

Mid-afternoon, the group pulled off again onto an island camp to take a stretch, pay attention to nature, and hear some more instructions for the next phase of the journey. Andeep warned them of rapids in their next river run. "You may wonder why we've had you wear life jackets up until now when everything was so peaceful," he said. "The colour makes it easy for us to keep track of you, but if you don't follow our lead exactly at each of the rapids ahead you'll be needing the life jackets for more than just looking pretty. Lesson three: Do exactly what you see us doing."

Fifteen minutes into the river run Vincent could hear the distinctive roar of rough water ahead. The open fields framing the river banks now rose on both sides to form a long narrow canyon with steep rock cliffs on either side. Up until now the conversation with Stephen had been mostly about the scenery they were seeing separated by long periods of silent awe. The chatter floating across the water from some of the other canoes may have been more but Vincent relished the comfort of the silent peace displayed in his own boat.

When Andeep motioned the group toward the right side of the river the six canoes flowed into single file without too much hesitation. After Andeep and Marshall there was Michael and Matthew, Navid and Darius, Maxwell and Toby, Vincent and Stephen with Hanny and Jimmy at the tail.

Vincent dug his paddle deeper into the water to slow things down as he watched those ahead of him take the rapids. The guides shot through without a problem. The Harrises followed and although there was a moment of panic as they had a near miss on a rock they also got through unscathed. The Samadis stayed too close to the cliff wall and several times appeared to have to push off with their paddles to get back into the main stream.

Vincent was watching the Njoroge's wild ride when the Prakash canoe shot past him. "We'll show you how it's done," yelled Hanny as he and Jimmy dug in their paddles.

Stephen caught a spurt of adrenaline and dug in his paddle as well. "C'mon dad," he yelled. "We can't let them beat us."

Vincent's paddle in the water resulted in the canoe jerking sideways a bit and the father and son moved at a dangerous angle into the rapids when they finally reached the crucial passage point. The Njoroges overshot their path and ended up in a fast-flowing rapid right in the middle of the river.

The guides began yelling instructions from ahead while Hanny Prakash was yelling from behind. This seemed to confuse Toby. He held out his paddle to keep from hitting a boulder and instead had the paddle knocked out of his hands.

Vincent was so busy watching the near disaster that he didn't watch his own path clearly enough. He missed a crucial paddle dig and before he knew it his world was nothing but water. He felt himself helplessly grabbed by a power beyond his control and hurled forward. He felt himself bounce off a rock and for a moment felt his foot wedge along the bottom. He pulled hard and fought for the surface to get some air.

Before he knew it the lifejacket had pulled him up and out of his watery grave. To his relief he saw Stephen bobbing along just ahead and the canoe floating sideways about fifteen feet away. In less than a minute he saw the canoe of Andeep and Marshall blocking their path and extending paddles for them to grab.

"Just hang on until we get through this canyon," Marshall instructed. "We'll get you up on the bank and let you put your gear back together. Just ignore the cold. You'll be okay. Once you survive a few dunks it helps with your fear of the river. Just hang onto the side for a minute. We're just going to snag your canoe and make sure we've got everything. Lesson four: Always keep your eye and mind on the leader."

Vincent perched on the edge of the craft and watched Andeep reach out and grab the capsized canoe. He already had the two stray paddles laying in the bottom of his own boat. Two minutes later Andeep called to him again. "Okay, we're through the worst. Just let go and drift downstream until the bank opens up. Swim your way to the right side and we'll meet you there."

Father and son released their grip and enjoyed the free float in the rushing current. They were surprised to see Maxwell and Toby standing waist deep in the shallow water near their landing spot. Their canoe was tugging at them from the rope tether which Maxwell had around his wrist.

Maxwell had a huge smile on his face. "House-Man, thanks for the support. Look what I caught. I gotta teach this boat how to float. This is one chilly bath. Give me the Indian Ocean any day."

Vincent helped Stephen find his footing as he moved toward shore and then waded toward Maxwell and helped him tug the reluctant craft into the shallows so they could beach it. He was glad for the warm sun overhead as he emerged onto solid ground again.

The rest of the group landed without incident and began to tell their renditions about what they had seen and experienced. Hanny was quick to talk about the look of terror on Vincent's face when he emerged out of the water. "You should have seen your face," he said. "I needed a video camera. And Njoroge! What a hoot. I thought I was watching a winner on the funniest home videos show."

The two fathers and two sons who had experienced the unforgiving power of the river quickly retrieved their packs and changed their clothing. The rest of the crew took time to wander into the bushes and to pull out snacks and munch. There was something about the outdoors that made a man hungry. Especially when his latest adventure had brought about a huge adrenaline spike.

Andeep and Marshall had very little to say other than to make sure that the canoes and paddles and equipment were all fine and that they were glad everyone was okay. "There are two more rapids a little rougher than this," Andeep warned. "And two not so bad. We've got 90 minutes until camp tonight. Stay close to the boat in front of you and don't fight the water. Go with it. Don't panic. You'll be okay."

Vincent double-checked to make sure Stephen was okay but all he saw was a huge smile as they prepared to launch back out onto the river.

CHAPTER EIGHTEEN

The next four rapids caused only minor problems for the group. On the roughest run, Michael and Matthew ended up with a canoe half filled with water but survived to the point where they could beach and empty their craft. Supper included Kraft Dinner and Pork and Beans so after clean up every father and son settled into his sleeping bag for the night. It had been a tiring first day for the city dwellers.

The second and third days through pristine wilderness contained more gliding through still water. The honk of a few early Canadian Geese sounded overhead on the final day but generally the birdsong exploded and echoed from the trees all around them.

During one river run, two gigantic bull moose stood munching in the grasses at water's edge and hardly moved as cameras were focused and clicked. On several occasions deer stared curiously from the edge of the tree line at the canoeists passing by. Vincent pointed out a pair of raccoons along the water's edge and Stephen was the first to notice a river otter.

At the next lake there was the collective feel of a giant cathedral and all conversation ceased with only the dipping of paddles breaking the silence.

The last night was to be spent in a cabin as Andeep and Marshall collected the canoes on their company vehicle for transport back up river again. The spinning whir of fishing lines sounded again and fresh trout provided a welcome treat for the hungry travellers.

A magnificent sunset topped off the adventure as fathers and sons alike sat on the shore watching the dance of colors playing against the bottoms of the clouds as the sun slowly descended out of sight. As they sat around the crackling fire and laughed and sang and recounted the first half of their adventure it seemed like the world they had once known was no more than a distant fairy tale.

Michael finished off the evening with a short story. The flickering flames set the perfect atmosphere for an adventure tale.

"Up until a few years ago in the land of the Cherokee every young man had to go through the rite of passage to become an official warrior. The father of the boy would take him deep into the forest and blindfold him. He would then tell his son to sit on a stump and spend the entire night without removing the blindfold. Only when the rays of the sun shone brightly through that blindfold could he take it off. The young man was told he could not cry out for help to anyone no matter what happened. If he survived this night, he would be a man. When this trial was over, he could never tell of his experience to another boy because each young one would have to become a man through his own effort."

Michael reached into a bag and drew out several patterned handkerchiefs. The crackle of the fire added mystery as he stood to his feet. "Now, I need the five fathers to take these blindfolds and to tie them tightly around the eyes of your son so he cannot see. Like those Cherokee boys your sons may be terrified at all the noises of the night that come their way. Their minds will conjure up all kinds of wild beasts that are hunting them down. The wind may blow, the wolves may howl, but this was the only way to become a man."

The five fathers took up the handkerchiefs and moved to stand behind their nervous sons.

"This was not one of the tasks I signed up for," Jimmy Prakash said.

"Me neither," Toby Njoroge agreed.

"That's okay," Michael said. "Since you've already chosen other tasks, let me tell you how this story ends. The young man would sit all night on that stump and when he saw the rays of the sun through his blindfold and took it off the first thing he would see would be the face of his own father. His dad would have been there with him through the whole night. I'm telling you this story so you know. Your dads will be with you through whatever you face on this trip. Don't give up no matter what."

As Vincent climbed into bed he tuned his ear to the night sounds and noted a few owls nearby. A distant howl of a wolf was answered by a closer bark of a coyote. His imagination told him that a nearby scratching, moaning and humphing sound was just a bear finding berries or exploring the garbage can nearby. He was glad that tonight was being spent inside a cabin. He did not want to be a father sitting by a blindfolded son deep in the forest somewhere.

Dawn broke far too early for the weary group but the adventure was only half way done. The next three days would be spent hiking and mountain climbing and this is where the wisdom of their supplies and packing would tell its own story.

Vincent kept his eye on the small grey cloud resting near the mountain top as Michael gathered the group after breakfast, supervised the clean-up, spread out the map of their hiking route, and led the team in prayer. He and Stephen checked through their supplies again, redistributed some of the weight, and then hoisted their packs to join the rest of the group.

The hikers had a fairly easy incline to manage during their first half hour. Spruce and pine trees formed the bulk of the growth around them. Vincent was pleased when Stephen was able to identify maple and birch and alder trees as well. He pointed out Dogwood, Cedar and Juniper trees.

He noticed that Maxwell and Toby were sticking close to hear his explanations as to what each tree could be used for and he realized that some of the things his father taught him long ago about herbal medicines did have some value at a time like this.

There was a group of oak trees seemingly out of place in this area and in a clearing they found small stands of fir and hemlock. There were cottonwood and wild cherries and laurel as well. The variety of coloring on bark and branch and leaf was the work of a master artist and while the talk on the trail was continuous it was not the irreverent jocularity that had marked the beginning of the adventure.

After that first thirty minutes the trail climbed at a serious angle. Within twenty minutes Vincent realized that his pack had somehow grown heavier. Jimmy asked for a break and the group halted and shuffled around in their packs for snacks and a little more weight shifting. Vincent was glad that Stephen didn't ask him to take any more. His son seemed determined to follow through on their agreed allotment.

Forty minutes later the group crested a hill and caught a breath-taking view of the lakes they had been canoeing through. That inspiration helped as the trail continued to wind upward at an unforgiving ascent. Vincent hoped the pictures he took could give Margaret some participation in what he and Stephen were experiencing. He could see through the lens that Stephen was weary but also happy with himself.

By the time the group stopped for lunch in an alpine meadow, Vincent was feeling like he had done all the climbing he really wanted to do. He was pleased that Matthew Harris seemed to be spending more time connecting with Stephen and the two seemed to have some special bonding going on. The trail had allowed different pairs of guys to walk together and there was a growing camaraderie developing among all of them.

Hanny and Jimmy both had a nap and seemed reluctant to pick up their pack and take the next leg of the journey. Vincent stepped in beside Hanny and tried to distract him with talk of his business and homeland and hobbies. That helped the next hours pass quicker.

At three-thirty, Michael Harris called the hikers into a group huddle. They were standing in a small clearing with two trails forking off of it. "We need to make a choice," he said. "According to this map there's a clearing we can camp in within half an hour if we take the trail to our left. If we take the trail to our right we have two more hours of walking before we can find a good spot. How tired are you? If we don't do the work today we will have to make it up tomorrow."

The group was split on its decision with six out of ten wanting to take the shorter route. Michael bowed to the majority decision and set off on the left trail. He called Vincent up to join him.

"Vincent," he said. "I know you spend most of your time in an office, but you and Stephen seem to be doing okay so far. I'm concerned about Hanny and Navid. Do you think we're going to be able to finish this climb in the time we set?"

Vincent pointed at the dark mass of clouds gathering overhead. "I'm more concerned right now about whether we can get to camp and set up in time before that rain comes," he said. "I think we've made the commitment to do this task together. The fathers and the sons need to see we're going to support them no matter what happens. If we have to take an extra day then we just need to take an extra day. I admit this was a lot easier to plan on paper than to do in real life."

Michael nodded. "I guess I'm too much of a type A," he said. "I've noticed the clouds. The weather forecast didn't have anything about thunder showers in this area but there's no doubt that we're about to get soaked soon. You're right. Let's pick up the pace and get set up the best we can."

Vincent called back to the others and pointed out the clouds. The threat above energized the group enough to get them moving. Within twenty-five minutes they had reached the clearing where tents were permitted. Michael walked around making sure that each tent was in a suitable location to avoid any flooding that might come.

Ground sheets and tents and tarps had barely been set in place before the first big drops began to fall. The next five hours were an awesome display of thunder and lightning and torrential downpours. Each father and son huddled in their own tent and ate cold snacks and provisions. After talking over the day Vincent and Stephen settled into a comfortable silence of reading by flashlight and journaling their thoughts of the adventure so far.

Vincent turned to Stephen and smiled. "I'm proud of you son," he said. "You're acting like a man more every day."

Stephen smiled back. "Thanks, Dad! I'm feeling more like a man every day."

When Vincent struggled out of his tent to find a tree first thing in the morning he walked out into a sea of mud. The clouds had drifted on by and the sun was stretching its first rays over the tips of the eastern peaks but hiking today was going to be a challenge.

This was the day set aside for some significant rock climbing as part of their testing. He wondered if they would have to forego some of their plans.

When he got back to camp Njoroge and Michael were huddled together over a small camp stove. Njoroge noticed him first. "Vince, Mansion Man, If I knew you were first up I'd have stopped trying to do this women's work. How am I supposed to make coffee when I've never done it before? Why do you think I've been sleeping in lately? If your bladder is gladder then come on and help us."

Vincent heard Hanny calling out from his tent. "Hey, Maxwell, tell me why your coffee always tastes like dirt? Wanna know why? 'Cause it was fresh ground this morning. Get it? Fresh ground – dirt?"

Njoroge retorted quickly. "Hanny, you don't have to worry about drinking my coffee. There's only mud out here and you can make your own brew if you want something good."

Maxwell next turned to Vincent. "What did you do with the furnace, man? This is summer and I've got icicles growing out my nostrils. We should have added a fur parka and ten pairs of socks to that list of things. The only reason I'm making coffee is so I can get warm again."

Breakfast took a significant amount of time to organize that morning and clean up took even longer. Every tent and tarp and groundsheet was caked in mud spatters from the heavy downpour. Michael gave suggestions on cleaning but in the end each father and son had to sort out how they were going to carry their messy shelters to the next stop. The spirit of several members of the group was far different than it had been just one night before.

CHAPTER NINETEEN

The trail was definitely soggier and took more effort in some parts. In parts where the trees hung over the path the moisture continued to drop onto the hikers. There were some drawbacks to taking a journey through such a densely forested area of the country.

The original plan had been to do the rock climb mid-morning but the group didn't reach the site until an hour and a half after lunch. The rock face was still wet from the previous night's storm and Michael called a huddle of the group to talk about their options.

"This is where we're scheduled to do our rock climb," he said. "The problem is we're four hours behind on our trip and the rock face is wet and could be dangerous. I'm suggesting we skip this part just to be safe."

"Dad," Matthew said. "How are we going to feel like we're men if we skip part of the task we agreed to? If we're careful we should be able to do this. We do wall climbs at the gym all the time and this can't be that much different."

"I agree," Jimmy said. "I think we can do this. Stephen, Darius, Toby… we're the ones who have to live with this. Do you think we can do this?"

Vincent watched Stephen bow to the peer pressure and nod his head. "I'd like us to think about this one more time," he said. "I know we've been revving up this man talk thinking about Cherokee warriors and all that, but being a man should also mean being wise enough to make changes when we need to. Can we look at the wall a little more and test it out a bit to see if it's safe enough. The last thing we want to do is to have a serious injury so far from help."

"I think we should at least look at that wall," Njoroge agreed. "If you boys think you can do it fine but I don't want to be the one at the bottom trying to catch you if you fall."

One by one the fathers and sons found rocks or grassy spaces to lay down their packs. They gathered at the bottom of the cliff face and looked way up. Matthew Harris was the first to take a trial run at the lower part of the rock climb and twelve feet up announced that he thought he could do it.

The other boys felt the pressure and stood back to watch.

Michael Harris announced. "Now, if anyone does not want to do this, I think any of your dads will understand."

Vincent moved to Stephen's side and said clearly, "you don't have to do this son."

"You'll be with me, right dad?" Stephen asked without taking his eyes off of Matthew.

"I'll be with you either way," Vincent said.

"I'm going next," Stephen said as he moved to the rock face.

The rock face rose for about thirty feet before a significant ledge allowed a climber to rest and Matthew seemed to reach that space without too much difficulty. Stephen waited for Matthew's wave and then started up. He too reached the space without too much trouble.

Jimmy had climbed about ten feet when a rock he was standing on dislodged and he lost his grip and came falling back. Both Hanny and Michael were there to catch him. Jimmy was shaken but determined so he chose a slightly different route and tried again. This time he made it. Toby also made the climb as did Darius.

The second half of the climb involved about fifty feet of climbing and this was the part that appeared to be wetter and less manageable. Matthew chose his route and started his ascent. Ten feet up he slipped and fell to the ledge where the other boys waited. For a second it looked like he would roll right over the edge and fall the thirty feet to where the fathers were standing but several of the boys grabbed onto him.

"Dad, we need the first aid kit," Stephen yelled. "Matthew gashed his knee."

Vincent raced to his backpack and pulled out the first aid kit. He used a carabineer to attach it to his waist strap and headed for the rock face. Michael was already climbing up to be with his son. Vincent didn't have time to think about what he was doing and slowly worked his way up the rock face noting where the boys had found firm footing and handholds.

Within three or four minutes he hoisted himself over the lip of the ledge and rolled into a small puddle of water that had pooled there. The group was gathered around Matthew and Michael was already cleaning the area around the wound. Vincent handed him the kit and watched as the father patched up his son.

When the job was done, he stood up and surveyed the scenery. "Wow, you can sure see a lot from up here. Congratulations! You men have successfully done your rock climbing. Let's check this one off and give ourselves a chance to make it to the camp tonight."

None of the boys put up an argument so the group worked their way down repelling on ropes that Matthew had set up for anyone who needed them. Njoroge and Hanny were quick to hug their sons when they touched ground again. Everyone seemed relieved to be past this section of the task.

Michael checked Matthew's knee one more time and then everyone hoisted their packs back on and set off on the next part of the trail. The next hour of the trail broke across the ridge of a mountain and the views were stunning all around.

Twice, the group had to traverse a long scree caused by avalanches. Toby lost his footing once and only the rope connected to the carabineer at his waist kept him from sliding all the way down the loose gravel and dirt.

The level of anxiety elevated after the incidents with Matthew and Toby. The extra caution slowed progress even more. The group skipped their afternoon break and pressed on to reach their designated rest spot.

The sun set before they made it and in the fading light Michael called the group together again. "We have an hour and a half to go," he said. "We can push on or we can try and set up a rough camp in the next clearing we come to."

"Let's stop!" Toby said. "My ankle got twisted back there and I'm having trouble walking. I'm okay if we rough it out here somewhere."

"Look at all the stars," Njoroge said. "I'm all for setting up and letting Vincent tell us what we're seeing up there. You can't see all this and deny the Creator."

Vincent spoke up. "Njoroge, I learned those star charts a long time ago. That doesn't mean I still remember them all. Sometimes all those star formations blur together when there's so many showing."

"Okay," Michael said. "Next clearing we stop. Let's keep moving until we get there."

Twenty minutes later they reached a small clearing in the lee of a mountain bluff. Shrubs and tree branches were recruited to assist in the setting up of covered shelters and the muddy tents were erected for the night. Some quick pre-packaged provisions were shared around and supper was done.

Vincent was glad for the mat that cushioned some of the rough places under his tent. Stephen was asleep before his father even had the chance to debrief the day.

As Vincent crawled into his sleeping bag he heard a blood curdling scream. Even Stephen woke up.

"Help!" It was Jimmy's voice. "My dad fell over the cliff. Help!"

Vincent unzipped his tent and raced out without even putting on his shoes. Michael and Njoroge were standing beside Jimmy near the embers of a fire.

"My dad went out to go to the bathroom," he said. "He let me keep the flashlight and kept walking. He just disappeared over that edge. We gotta help him quick."

Michael walked to the edge of the clearing and called down into the darkness. "Hanny! Hanny? Can you hear me?"

No sound was heard and Jimmy began to cry. Vincent went back for his shoes and put his dirty feet into them. He grabbed his stronger flashlight and took it out to the edge where he could shine it down. A faint reflection of blue rested in a tree branch forty feet below. There seemed to be no movement.

"Get the ropes," Michael called. "I'm going down. Vincent, I need you down as well. The rest of you wait until I can tell you what we need."

Michael tied off a pair of ropes to a tree, formed a loop around his foot with one of them and then stepped over the edge. He worked his way slowly down the cliff face until he had reached the tree which held Hanny. "Vincent, come!" he called.

Vincent had taken a helmet light from Michael and put it around his head. That, plus the flashlight fastened to his waist strap helped him see enough to slowly work his way down. It seemed like hours but he made it without incident. Michael had already started climbing up the tree which hung precariously over a deep ravine.

"We can't shake that branch and dislodge him," Michael said. "I'm going to try and attach a rope to some part of his body so he doesn't go any farther. Maybe I'll need you to go out for help. Do you think you can find your way enough so that you can get cell phone contact? All I know is that you need to go southwest from here to get near the camp. You can read the stars, right? Hanny needs some serious help. Can you do it?"

Vincent looked high into the heavens at the roadmap that the Creator had spread out for all to read. He began to see and know. "I can do it," he said.

"Then go as quick as you can," Michael said. "Hanny's life may depend on it."

Vincent struggled to get himself up the slippery surface of the muddy cliff and relied on the group above to help lift him over the edge. Navid prepared to take his place below with Michael and Vincent set off into the bush with the flashlight lighting up the ground and the stars lighting up the sky.

CHAPTER TWENTY

Within half an hour it became obvious that the path was veering away from the direction Vincent needed to go. At this time of night he did not want to go bush barging so he kept pressing on in hopes that the trail would turn in a more favourable direction. He arrived at the camp that had been their original destination but no one was there.

He sat on a stump at the edge of the camp and looked up at the stars and prayed for help. Nothing obvious like a meteor shower, shooting star, lunar eclipse or flashing satellite gained his attention. He just felt a sense of confidence about carrying on.

Twenty minutes later he came to a fork in the trail. The main trail was well worn but continued moving away from where he needed to go. The side trail appeared to be slightly overgrown but curved definitely toward the southwest. With another silent prayer the realtor took the smaller path.

Within fifteen minutes the path began to rise steeply. He felt himself breathing hard and even panting as he stretched himself to grab tree branches and roots to keep moving upward. A good forty minutes passed before he found himself in a clearing on top of a hill.

He offered up another short prayer and pulled out his cell phone. The lighted face showed a faint signal. He dialed 911 and waited. There was no response.

He flashed his light around and saw that he could still climb another hill that would get him another fifty feet. Without hesitation he took the option. When he tried the phone again there was a slightly stronger signal. He dialed 911 again. This time he heard a faint voice…"911, Where can I direct your call… fire, ambulance, police?"

"I don't know," Vincent said. "We have an injured man on top of a mountain near Black's peak and he's fallen off a cliff and is hanging in some tree branches over a ravine. We don't know what to do but we need help."

"I'll put you through to Search and Rescue," the operator said. "Your call will be monitored and I will stay on the line with you until we know what is happening. Please describe in as much detail where you are and how we can reach you. Your call signal is very weak."

Vincent was on the phone for fifteen minutes with the Search and Rescue coordinator before it was decided that a helicopter with a search light would be sent his way. "Please find a way to light up the area where you are near Black's Peak and we'll try and lower someone down to be with you. Our team is being assembled to leave here in just a few minutes. Flight time may be thirty to forty minutes. Please keep us in touch and return to your group. If our signal cuts out we will be looking for your light."

The signal did cut out before Vincent had even descended from his hill. He pocketed his cell phone and tried to move as quickly as possible down the steep grade of the mountain he had been climbing. Twice he got tangled in roots or vines and fell down a significant number of feet but still he kept pushing himself. His right knee was hurting bad from his last fall.

When he reached the fork in the trail where the path was wider and smoother he tried to jog and then walk as fast as he could manage. His lungs were bursting and his knees were crying out in protest but he refused to give in. There was a band of brothers depending on him.

Instinctively, he kept glancing skyward and charting his course even though there weren't any options. There was no sign of a helicopter by the time he reached the empty campsite. He started to move his flashlight from ground to sky as often as possible just in case. His watch told him forty-five minutes had passed.

It had been almost three hours since he had scaled the cliff from where Hanny lay and his mind began to create frightening scenarios about what reality he would find when he arrived back at camp.

He estimated that he had ten minutes to go when he jogged unsteadily across a clearing. His flashlight picked up a set of eyes off to the side and when he shone his beam on the owner of those eyes he saw a grizzly tearing at a stump. The bear turned in his direction but Vincent found a level of adrenaline he didn't know he had and ran down the trail ahead.

For the next five minutes he was certain he heard the thumping footsteps and heavy growls of a grizzly right behind him. He was sure he had heard somewhere that he was supposed to lie down and play dead but he was too scared to even slow down.

He heard the helicopter about the same time he heard the shouts of the group ahead of him. He began to yell "shine your lights into the sky, shine your lights into the sky." He was so out of breath that he wasn't even sure anyone could hear him. When he turned the last corner of the trail his son Stephen was waiting for him. Vincent felt like he had just completed a marathon. The father and son embraced in a strong bear hug and then Vincent collapsed.

"Help us!" Stephen yelled. "My dad's collapsed. Help us!"

Jimmy and Matthew arrived to help Stephen lift his dad and drag him back to the group. Stephen lifted a canteen to Vincent's lips and called someone to bring a blanket.

Vincent collected his wits and remembered his mission. "Everyone has to shine their lights together toward the helicopter," he whispered hoarsely. "They need to see where we are."

The helicopter passed by twice to the south of the group without stopping. At Vincent's instructions they moved together as a group and shone their lights into the sky toward the helicopter.

Five minutes later they could see the craft moving in their direction. A blinding spotlight turned the night to day. The boys began cheering. Only then did Vincent notice that none of the fathers were nearby.

"Where are the others?" Vincent asked Stephen.

"Matthew's dad tried to tie ropes around Jimmy's dad on that tree down there," shouted Stephen over the noise of the helicopter. "He got one rope around his ankle and one around a wrist but then the branch cracked. The other dads are down there trying to keep that branch from falling all the way down. I think I heard that Jimmy's dad was talking to the others and trying to be still."

Vincent dragged himself, with Stephen's help toward the cliff edge and watched the daring rescue attempt.

The hovering craft opened a hatch, dropped a rope and a solo rescuer slid down to join the boys on the upper level. The spotlight was clearly showing everyone how precarious Hanny's attachment to the cracked tree limb was. The wash from the propeller blades of the helicopter was threatening to bend the branch even more.

Another rescuer slid down the rope and joined the first. The two surveyed the situation and quickly scaled down to join the fathers. The helicopter moved up a little higher to protect the operation below.

A third dark figure emerged on the dangling rope and slowly hovered in place as he was moved toward Hanny. A basket of some kind was also lowered until it was parallel with the dangling rescuer. The two rescuers on the ground were providing instructions through their contact radios to the pilot and the rescuer on the rope.

When the hanging rescuer was within reach of Hanny he quickly tied off the branch and moved the basket into place beside Hanny. A pair of connecting ropes were tossed between the hoverer and the two rescuers on the cliff ledge. They used these ropes to steady the swing of the basket. The cracking of the branch was hard to hide any longer.

Vincent held his breath as the man on the rope made a desperate grab for Hanny and pulled him into the basket. The tree branch splintered until it was hanging and swinging by its bark and not much else. Only the ropes tethering it to the helicopter kept it from plunging into the ravine.

Michael and Navid were still holding the ropes that bound Hanny to the branch and they were almost pulled over the edge when the tree branch cracked. They were fortunate to have the two rescuers grab them and slash the ropes they had tied around their waist.

The dangling rescuer who now held Hanny also cut the ropes that bound him to the branch and with that the pair swung away from the cliff and out into the darkness. Vincent could feel a scream rising in his throat as the basket with Hanny vanished from under the light of the spotlight.

The realtor could see the helicopter swing away and rise up. He couldn't believe what he had just seen. The spotlight moved toward the space where he lay and continued to focus on him. He was blinded and unable to move.

Two pairs of hands grabbed at him and urged him to come. It was the rescuers who had climbed the cliff. The men pulled him to the edge of the clearing into a darker space and Vincent soon saw the other fathers and boys huddle nearby.

There was constant chatter across the radio phones and then the helicopter was back and lowering the basket onto the ground. The third rescuer released the cable that tied the basket and was immediately joined by the other two who appeared to be applying first aid on Hanny.

Five minutes later one of the rescuers joined the group of fathers and sons. "Well done, men," he said. "That was close. I'm Captain Caleb Southerland at your service. We're going to have to fly your friend in for some help. I'm afraid the rest of you are going to have to hang in here and make your way out tomorrow. Is everyone else okay?"

Tobey mentioned his ankle and the rescuer examined it. "Normally, I'd tell you that you'll be fine in a couple of days.

Just wrap it and use some crutches to keep the weight off of it. Out here that won't work so well. If the others are okay, we'll take you with us. It'll be a little tricky doing a double load with the basket but give us time. We've got to do this quickly as our run time allowance is getting pretty narrow."

Captain Southerland huddled with the other two and a call was made for the chopper's return. The craft hovered closer and Vincent and Stephen held on tightly to a small sapling. Two of the tents were blown off into the bushes and no one went after them for the moment.

When the Captain returned to the group it was Njoroge who spoke first. "Captain, please tell Mr. Prakash that if he will look after my son then I'll look after his. We'll all be fine. Please tell our families. I've left the phone numbers with Toby."

The rescue operation and basket lift took less than ten minutes and then the helicopter's blinding spot light shut off and the craft floated away as if it had been some UFO in their dreams.

The fathers and sons stood still in the darkness as their eyes adjusted again and finally one flashlight and then another was turned on. "I guess we better get our tents back and settle down for the night," Vincent said. "Well done, Michael, everyone, well done."

"Well done yourself," Michael said. "If it wasn't for you finding a way to connect with the Search and Rescue we'd be facing some pretty serious consequences right now. I don't know how far you went or what you had to do but I thank God for giving you the strength."

"I also want to thank my Father in heaven," Vincent said.

"But I also want to publicly say a thanks to my earthly father. His persistence in teaching me about the stars was something I always thought was a waste of time. Tonight, it made all the difference. Nothing we learn is ever wasted."

CHAPTER TWENTY-ONE

Vincent found it hard to get comfortable and sleep that night. It was after 4 am by the time the camp was back in order and everyone had talked through the adventure they had just experienced. His body hurt badly and his adrenaline surge was still flowing through every fibre of his being.

Stephen broke the silence from his sleeping bag. "Dad, I'm so proud of you. You saved Mr. Prakash's life. Did that grizzly really almost get you?"

Vincent had retold the details of his story and he had listened to the stories of those who had stayed behind. The terror of the bear was still very fresh in his memory.

"All I know," Vincent said, "is that God gave me the adrenaline I needed to get back here. I was about ready to give up when I saw that bear. I've never been so scared in all my life. I was sure he was just a few feet behind me all the way."

"I'm glad I didn't see him when I met you," Stephen said. "When you hugged me and fell I thought I'd lost you. That was one of the scariest times in my life as well."

"We're both here," Vincent said. "Tomorrow we'll summit by lunch and try to make it down to the last cabin so we can get picked up for our ride home. We're almost there. I am really seeing what kind of a young man you are and I'm proud of you too."

Despite the horrific experiences of the previous evening the group broke camp by 8 am and hit the trail that would lead them to the summit. Each of them had taken time to look over the precipice to see the place where Hanny had fallen. The tree branch was no longer in place and Vincent felt himself shudder when he realized the implications of what could have been.

A few hundred yards down the path Michael called back over his shoulder. "Bear scat," he said. "Looks like a big bear was here recently. Vincent, that bear may have been closer than you think. I'd hate to have anything else happen. Keep your eyes open everyone."

Njoroge and Jimmy fell into step with each other for the first few minutes and then comfortably changed walking partners as had happened throughout the adventure. Jimmy moved up next to Vincent. "I wanted to thank you for all you did to rescue my dad last night," Jimmy said. "I don't know what I'd do without him. I used to be embarrassed sometimes around him with his corny humour and all. He wasn't always around when I needed him but he's really tried with these 12 Tasks. I always thought Stephen was the lucky guy to have a dad like you and I know he is. But thanks to you, I realize I have a chance to feel like I'm pretty lucky to have my dad too. Anyway, I just wanted to say thanks."

Vincent put his arm around Jimmy's shoulders. "Your dad is a good man," he said. "And you're becoming a great young man yourself. God has been so good to each of us. Don't forget that when more hard things come. Remember how much you love your dad right now and don't let go of that. He's so proud of you as well. Keep him proud. Climb this mountain for both of you."

Just after ten the group cleared the forest line and saw the rising summit above them. Vincent felt the momentum drain out of him. The climb would take at least four hours up and then they'd have an eight-hour trek to the final cabin. He wasn't sure he had the endurance to do this task.

Njoroge stepped up next to Vincent. "This is for my son," he said. "If this little hill is all it takes to make us men, then we better get this done. That sun up there is not going to get any cooler with us standing still."

Michael huddled the group one more time. "Let's leave our packs to the side of the trail in a tree so we don't attract bears," he said. "It looks like the snowcap has receded enough that we'll only be in the white stuff for an hour or two. Bring your warm stuff and make sure your footwear is solid. I'll give you five minutes to hoist your packs and sort your stuff then we need to get moving. We'll be fortunate to get to the cabin by mid-night. Say your prayers and keep your feet moving."

"Shouldn't we bring extra rope and tie ourselves off to each other once we hit the snowline?" Vincent asked.

"Good point," Michael answered. "Fathers, grab all your rope, get enough water, and let's do this. And please don't forget your cameras. This is one picture you don't want to forget."

The group hit the snowline just before one in the afternoon and they stopped for fifteen minutes to eat lunch and rest. The rope was connected through carabineers to each person in the line and the last phase of the task was underway.

The trail wound its way up in the shaded side of the rock cliff and the snow was icy and slippery underfoot. Michael took the lead in creating toe holds for the group but then he tired and gave way to Matthew for the next five minutes. When he tired, Navid took over and then Njoroge.

Vincent was in the lead when the line of exhausted climbers crested the last steep rise and saw the last gentle slope to the peak. New energy burst through them and the boys began to push ahead to beat the fathers to the goal. The vista would have been breathtaking on any given day if they hadn't already been almost breathless from the effort of the climb and the thinner level of oxygen at this height.

Cameras were produced and pictures were taken of the boys and then the fathers and then each father and son. Njoroge and Jimmy posed together with both of them holding two arms up for the partner they had climbed for.

Vincent marvelled at the scenery of a necklace of pristine lakes connected by the strand of rivers that stretched as far as they could see. The mountain range stretched on to the horizon with several of the peaks still boasting snow despite the summer.

It was three-thirty when the group began sliding slowly down the hill toward home. They'd climbed for three days to spend fifteen minutes on top of a mountain. They had held a small ceremony certifying themselves as men and saying a series of short prayers for Hanny and Toby. There was still eight hours of downward hiking before the real end could be celebrated.

Several of the boys took turns sliding for short distances down the snow field but with steep ravines all around it was very short and controlled and a rope was still attached to a father who held on just in case.

When they conquered the last of the snow the boys seemed to instinctively take the lead on their own. Freed from the rope harnesses they made their way confidently down the path.

Vincent was glad to see that Stephen appeared just as confident as the others in his footsteps and pace.

By the time the fathers reached the tree where the packs were hanging the boys had already brought the packs down and reorganized their own loads. The fathers stopped to rest, pack, adjust their gear, drink and eat a few snacks. It was six o'clock and darkness would be falling soon.

The next hours were mind-numbing for Vincent as the trip began to take its toll on him. With little rest, with the bumps and bruises from his falls, with the significant pain in his right knee, he knew he was hobbling and starting to fall behind.

The realtor could hear the voices below and see the flashes of light through the trees but he was starting to feel unable to hold his light properly and suddenly he was face down on the ground. The pain in his hands and chest was intense and he just wanted to rest his head on his arm and sleep.

He thought of Margaret and what a good life they'd had together. He thought of Stephen and how proud he was that his son had proved his manhood through these tasks. He'd lived a good life. Hanny was safe because of his sacrifice. He just needed to rest.

CHAPTER TWENTY-TWO

Vincent heard Stephen's voice somewhere in the darkness. All he could do is grunt his acknowledgement. A few minutes later a light shone in his face. Still, he didn't move. A hand began shaking his shoulder and a voice was screaming into his ear.

The realtor felt his pack being removed and he was flipped over onto his back. He just wanted to sleep. He felt someone reaching into his mouth and then pushing on his chest. His mind clicked in as to what was happening and he began to laugh.

"What's so funny?" Stephen asked. "Dad, are you okay? Dad, don't do this to me now. We're almost there. This isn't funny."

Vincent forced his eyes open and then shut them as the flashlight beam was so bright. "Take the light away and let me see," he said. "I'm just tired. I fell. Sorry, I just need to rest."

"Dad, I thought you were dead," Stephen said.

"Where did you learn CPR?" Vincent asked.

"Remember, you made me go to that lifeguard course last summer?" Stephen said. "We had to learn all about it then. Dad, you have to get up. The rest of the group doesn't even know we're gone yet. They're all like zombies down there."

Vincent rolled himself over and got up on his hands and knees. "Give me a chance to visit the bushes for a minute and I'll be right with you," he said. "We can't have zombies showing up at the cabin when they're expecting men."

Once Vincent was ready to move on Stephen exchanged backpacks with him to lighten his load. There was no protest from the father's lips. He just put his hand on the shoulder of his son and began lurching down the winding trail through the woods. Twenty minutes later they heard Michael coming up the trail toward them calling.

Stephen answered the call and soon Michael had relieved Vincent of his pack and stepped in place of Stephen to steady Vincent as he stumbled ahead. Fifteen minutes later they met the group lying on their packs beside the trail. None of them even flinched when Michael shone his light on them.

Michael pulled out his whistle and blew it. The effect was immediate on the nappers. "We have four hours," Michael said. "It'll be morning by then. The van is supposed to pick us up at 8 am. Do you want to rest now for twenty minutes and get there just in time or do you want to push on and get a shower before we go?"

The thought of a shower after a week in the wilderness proved to be a good enough incentive for the majority of the group to get them to their feet.

"I want to get back to see my son," Njoroge said.

"And I want to see my dad," Jimmy added.

"Let's do it!" Michael said.

The men took turns providing a shoulder for Vincent on the steeper drops of the trail but he soon began to find his rhythm and with an hour left he was feeling a new energy pulling him on.

When Vincent looked ahead he noticed that Stephen had taken the lead and was setting the pace for the others. He felt a pride surging in his chest and determined that he wasn't going to let down his son again.

The first light of dawn broke through the treetops with half an hour to go. Birdsong grew in volume and a new life seemed to fall like mist on all of them. "His mercies are new every morning," Njoroge said loudly.

"As your day, so will your strength be," Navid said.

"The Lord is our refuge and strength, an ever present help in time of trouble," Vincent chimed in.

"This is the day that the Lord has made. I will rejoice and be glad in it," Darius said.

Navid rubbed his hand proudly through his son's hair then said, "Man, you need a shower."

When they broke out of the timber into a gravel parking area near the cabin they saw the van pulling in to pick them up.

"I did not come all this way not to get my shower," Michael said. "Spread out, young men first. Let's get cleaned up before we get taken out with the trash. I'll stall the driver. First, let's get a picture so we can see before and after."

The driver took their picture and thirty-five minutes later eight freshly groomed conquerors plumped their weary bodies into their seats and promptly began to doze off. Vincent was one of the few who couldn't really sleep outside his own bed and he surveyed each individual with admiration.

He saw Michael looking back at him from the front passenger's seat. "Maybe we were too ambitious in our task," Vincent said.

"Maybe," Michael replied. "But they will never forget this trip and they will know without a doubt that they are men. And they will recognize heroes like you can come disguised as real dads. I think we're onto something here. I'd love it if you could help me with the next group of dads who might want to do this. You've got a special son there. Maybe he could help with mentoring some of the younger ones."

"Let's get through today first," Vincent said. "These tasks have taught me so much about being a man and how it has to do with our character as much as anything. Even though I didn't get to do something like this with my dad, I sure am glad I got to do it with my son."

"I was thinking," Michael said. "You may only have one son to do this with but there are single moms in our church who have no men for their sons to do this with. You and I could be like substitute dads for a year while these young guys go through their tasks. Our sons could be like big brothers. I can see this being radical for young guys before they get pulled into gangs and into questionable friendships. Pray about it."

"I will," Vincent said. "It sounds like something that could change the whole youth culture of a church or neighbourhood. You realize of course that we've got to prove ourselves trustworthy if single moms and others are going to trust us with their boys."

"It always starts with trust," Michael said. "We all went a long way to start earning that trust by what we've done with our own sons. The next step is to have our individual manhood celebrations for each of these boys. I'd love to be one of the men who speak for Stephen if you'll have me."

"I wouldn't have it any other way," Vincent said. "I've

picked out eight men who speak words of affirmation and courage to Stephen. The one thing I haven't sorted out yet is that weekend away for the man talk and purity ring initiation."

"We'll get together next Saturday and talk about some of the next steps," Michael said. "Right now, we have done what we came to do. I'm giving my wife a call and then Hanny. Maybe you should call Margaret. These guys aren't going to wake up even if a tornado came through here and took us all away to Kansas."

Vincent could tell that Margaret was pleased and relieved to get his call. She freely spoke about how Hanny and Toby had told everyone of his feat in getting the help that saved them on the mountain. Vincent felt an inward warmth at her love and praise. "I'm three hours away, honey," he said. "I'm bringing a young man home who is going to be hungrier than a bear. We'll probably sleep for a week but when I finally wake up, you're going to find yourselves with a new man in your life."

Vincent glanced back and saw Stephen watching him and smiling. He put a thumbs up for his son and Stephen did likewise. The teen years were still ahead but a major barrier had been crossed and a solid foundation of character had been built with the completion of the 12 Tasks of manhood.

The realtor from the city looked out the side window at the distant mountains which had tested him in every way he could imagine. One short scripture passage came to his mind. Psalm 121:1-2. "I lift up my eyes to the hills- where does my help come from? My help comes from the LORD, the Maker of heaven and earth."[1]

---

1   NIV

"Thank you, LORD," he said. He rested his head against the vibrating window and let the shadows of the past week slip away.

CHAPTER TWENTY-THREE

Five weeks after the adventure on the mountain, Vincent leaned casually against the portal of the living room and watched his son Stephen joking easily with the others in the room. The chrysalis of manhood had burst open and it was a wonder to behold.

The near fatal climb, which was the culmination of their 12 Tasks of Manhood, had bonded them closer. There was a confidence in the young man as he prepared for this day of recognition and celebration. A confidence Vincent still didn't feel in himself.

'Would the words he shared with his son this day be enough to affirm him yet challenge him to move ahead? What would the five other fathers in the room be thinking as he modeled the ceremony they all planned to have? How would he keep up the bond that had been formed when the intense pressures of work and peer groups and life's disappointments arrived to crowbar them apart?'

Maxwell Njoroge approached and enveloped him with a massive hug. "So, Mr. Real Estate Man, are you now a believer? All 12 Tasks done right on time."

"Njoroge. To tell you the truth, I'm glad we're done, but I'm still concerned about what comes next. Do you ever wonder if you can be enough for your son when there are so many others who impact his life?"

"That's the beauty of these 12 Tasks. We're a team. We're the village raising the child. We're doing this together."

"I guess I'm not so worried about my son. I'm more worried about me. I never went through anything to show I'd become a man. My son has made his mark. He can look back on this day, he can read everyone's affirmation, he can look at the videos and he can relive the memories. He can look at the ring on his finger. He'll know. I'm not sure what I have to help me."

"Vincent, brother, you are the daddy lion. Your cub is growling and prowling. He's doing what God designed him to do. He's being who God designed him to be. These 12 Tasks didn't just prove that Stephen in now a man. They proved that you are one too."

"I never thought of it that way. I was just doing what needed to be done."

"And that's the core of being a man."

Vincent accepted Njoroge's friendly fist bump and shoulder nudge and stepped over to the huddled group around Stephen. His son was retelling the drama of the last night on the mountain when two of the group had to be air lifted away.

"I'll never forget what my dad did for us," Stephen said. "Just to think, his dad taught him about the stars when he was young and that was what made all the difference. I can't wait to help my son go through his tasks. My dad says we're going to be world changers. I can't wait to see what God is creating for us next."

Vincent stepped away and bumped into Michael. The knowing look in his friend's eyes warmed him to the core.

"That boy sure is proud of his dad," Michael said.

"As I'm proud of him. I guess we better get this ceremony

underway. It looks like everyone is here."

Vincent gathered the group of fathers and sons and began his tribute to his son.

"On this day we are gathering not just as fathers and sons. We are gathering as men. Men who have triumphed over challenges we thought were once too great for our souls to face. Challenges which sucked the courage from our hearts. Challenges which threatened to sap our spirit of strength and hope. We are here, together. Changed.

"On this day, my son Stephen is stepping up to declare that he has finished his journey of the 12 Tasks of Manhood. He built up areas where he was strong. He developed areas where he was needing to grow. He learned new skills and accomplished significant feats of adventure.

"I am proud to see his love for God, for his neighbour, and for his family and friends. I am proud to see the way he has developed his heart, mind, soul and body. His mother, and I, together, wish to pass on a life verse for him.

"The verse is 1 Timothy 4:12. "Don't let anyone look down on you because you are young but set an example for the believer in your speech, your life, your love, your faith and your purity.[2]

This past weekend Stephen and I spent time talking through the importance of purity as a man. The ring he has is a reminder of the promises we made to support each other in this way."

The loud thumping and cheers of support brought a flush of red to Stephen's cheeks but it didn't suppress his grin.

Vincent stiffened his back, nodded in his son's direction, and continued.

---

2   NIV

"Two weeks ago, my good friend Maxwell Njoroge spent time talking with Stephen about his speech." More thumping and cheering. "Michael talked with Stephen last week about his love. Sam spoke on life and behaviour just a few days ago. Pastor Harris spoke to Stephen last Sunday night on faith. Each of you have had a crucial role to play.

"Today, I ask you to affirm your final words to a new young man among us. When you are done, Stephen will share a short response he had prepared. After that we'll review the highlights of his tasks and then we'll feast."

Stephen was sitting taller as each man shared his words of affirmation. A book of memories on the 12 Tasks was presented. Stephen shared from his heart and the day was done.

The ice-block within his soul melted away. 'Perhaps manhood was something that he would continue to grow into. Perhaps manhood was a lifelong journey for every son of a father. The important thing was getting started.'

QUESTIONS FROM THE BOOK TO CONSIDER

1. "When you think of your boys becoming men what characteristics do you want others to see in them? And how in our society will boys become this way?"
2. Is there hope for the future, confidence in the present and peace with the past for both father and son?
3. What are some of the ways that men and boys try to prove themselves?
4. What are the top 4-6 strengths you notice in each other?
5. What is one potential community outreach task you could do with other father/son teams to test out your chemistry and compatibility with others?
6. What is one positive thing you have seen each other accomplish but haven't shared your pride in words? Share it.
7. When you looked at the five areas of evaluation (spiritual, personal, financial, physical, sexual) how did both of you do in the areas mentioned? Can you discern any strength or growth area from these charts?
8. When you look at growth areas for the two of you which ones comes to mind?
9. What are some potential adventures you can imagine to engage in with other father and son teams?
10. What do you think is important to communicate during a father/son discussion on purity?
11. Who could you invite to have a say or impact on your son's journey?

OTHER BOOKS BY JACK TAYLOR

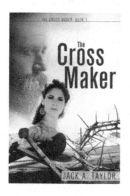 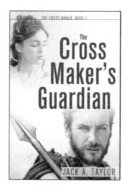 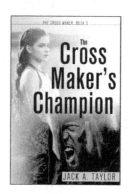

The award-winning Cross Maker series focuses on first-century Palestine as a hotbed of political, cultural and religious intrigue. Caleb ben Samson, a carpenter from Nazareth, and Sestus Aurelius, a Roman Centurion, both want peace. Can this unlikely partnership accomplish what nothing else has accomplished before? Can they bring peace through the power of the cross?

Katie Joy Delancey has staked her life on keeping the past and future away from her heart. Her MK past continues to test her faith and capacity for love. This series is about being discovered no matter who you are, where you've been or where you think you might be going. Can our past really be redeemed?

For more details visit: thecrossmaker.ca or jackataylor.ca search the book titles on Amazon.

Made in the USA
Middletown, DE
29 June 2025

77645479R00086